SANDPIPER

BY THE SAME AUTHOR

AISHA
IN THE EYE OF THE SUN

SANDPIPER

Ahdaf Soueif

BLOOMSBURY

Excerpt from 'Sandpiper' from *The Complete Poems 1927–1979* by
Elizabeth Bishop. Copyright © 1979, 1983 by Alice Helen Methfessel.
Reprinted by permission of Farrar, Straus & Giroux, Inc.

'Sandpiper' first appeared in *Granta* (1994), 'Chez Milou' in *Soho Square* (1988), 'The Water-Heater' (1982) and 'Melody' (1988) both appeared in the *London Review of Books*

First published in Great Britain 1996

This paperback edition published 1997

Copyright © 1996 by Ahdaf Soueif

The moral right of the author has been asserted

Bloomsbury Publishing Plc, 38 Soho Square, London W1V 5DF

A CIP catalogue record for this book
is available from the British Library

ISBN 0 7475 3081 5

10 9 8 7 6 5 4 3 2 1

Typeset by Hewer text Composition Services, Edinburgh
Printed in Great Britain by Cox & Wyman Ltd, Reading

The world is a mist. And then the world is
minute and vast and clear. The tide
is higher or lower. He couldn't tell you which.
His beak is focused; he is preoccupied,

looking for something, something, something.
Poor bird, he is obsessed!
The millions of grains are black, white, tan and grey,
mixed with quartz grains, rose and amethyst.

– Elizabeth Bishop, 'Sandpiper'

For Ricki

CONTENTS

MELODY

The scent of jasmine fills the air. It has been filling the air for the last month, I guess. Which is how you know the season is changing in this country. In this country the bougainvillaea blooms against the walls all the year round. The lizards dart out from under the stones and back in again. The mosquitoes buzz outside the netting and the pool-boy can be seen tending the pool every morning from eight to ten. We're not allowed to use the pool; us women, I mean. It's only for the kids – and the men of course. They can use anything. And they do. Use anything I mean. And I don't get to smell the jasmine that much either. You can only really smell it at night and I don't go out that much at night because of Wayne. Not that there's anywhere to go, you understand. Only shopping, or visiting in the compound. But even that I don't get

3

much of. Wayne sleeps at eight. If he doesn't get his twelve hours he's a real grouch all of the next day. And he has to wake up at half-past seven in the morning to catch the school bus. Now that's one thing I could never understand; why was the child never sent to school? She just kept her with her all the time. When we first came to this compound six months ago they were the first people I saw. The first residents, that is. You don't count the maintenance people and the garden-boys. We moved in on a Friday afternoon and the first thing we did was get right out again and drive up and down the road and I remember we said how convenient it was to have a grocer's, a newsagent, a flower-shop and a hospital right on our doorstep practically. Not that any of them looked like they were up to much but still they'd have to be better than nothing. And on the Saturday morning, as Wayne and I came back from the grocery store (Rich had gone to work, of course – that's my husband), we saw a woman and a child standing by the pool. The woman smiled, and Wayne ran over. I followed. Mind you, I thought she looked a bit tacky from the start, her hair was bronze, obviously dyed, and you could see the dark roots where it was growing out. She had quite a bit of eye make-up and her skirt was shorter than you normally see around here. She hadn't even bothered with an *abaya* which is normally OK on a compound but not with such a short skirt. The kid was very pretty though, and little Waynie fell for her straight away. She was a true blonde with natural fabulous curls. Her face was heart-shaped with a small *retroussé* nose and big blue eyes and she had drawn one of her mother's veils over her like a miniature *abaya*. It turned out she was only a couple of months older than Wayne. But she was much more self-conscious, self-possessed. Being a girl, I guess. Girls grow up quicker than boys. Well, Ingie, that was her name, the woman's I mean, chatted away – although you couldn't really call it chatting since her English is appalling – but she told me a bit about the compound and I asked where her kid went to school because I had to decide on a school for Waynie and she said Melody did not go to school. She said she had another baby, Murat, who was asleep upstairs just then, and she was keeping them together and teaching Melody how to read and write. She said, 'I like her with me.' I thought straight away that was wrong, although, of course, it wasn't for me to say, but the kid couldn't speak a word of English. She was very pretty and everything and in point of fact Wayne was standing there just staring at her all through our conversation. He was smitten. I think he just fell in love. Well, later that day when Wayne dropped his gun in the pool and I couldn't reach it and he's crying his head off, Ingie appears at her window and lowers a broomstick, yelling: 'Try this, try this.' So we got the gun out of the water and went upstairs to give her back her broomstick and Wayne just would not leave; he had to stay and play with Melody. I've never understood what the attraction was, quite frankly. She never played his kind of game. All she'd do was play with dolls and dress and

5

undress them and talk to them – in Turkish. While he watched. And once I went to collect him and found them both sitting on the bathroom floor with bare feet and wet clothes, 'washing' all the dolls' clothes. And Ingie just laughs and says, 'It is so hot.' Ingie's main thing is laughing. Laughing and clothes and make-up and dancing. And cooking. When we first moved in, she would come round, maybe twice a week, each time with some 'little thing' she had made: pastry, apple tart, pizza, whatever, things that take a lot of making. And little Melody was helping her. She also helped her, she said, make all those tiny doll's clothes for Barbie. I said, 'But you can buy them at Toyland for practically nothing,' and she laughed and shrugged and said, 'But I like.' And I guess she likes cooking three-course meals and a sweet for her husband every night and waiting on him too, no doubt. The way these Muslim women treat their husbands just makes me ill. They actually *want* to be slaves. Mind you, of course, that's probably how she got him in the first place. I thought it was a bit odd when I saw him: a great, big, tall man and obviously a lot older than her. And, laughing, she tells me that they (Ingie, Melody and Murat) are his second family. I pretend to be surprised but in point of fact Elaine had already told me (Elaine is my Scots friend – she's been here for almost four years and she knows everything), Elaine had told me he used to be married to an American woman and he'd lived in Denver for twenty years. They had two boys and he looked after them and did everything else as well. The wife worked and she had, like, a strong personality and naturally she wouldn't do anything in the house. I have a lot of sympathy with that. I mean housework and me are not best friends. I'd rather read a book. I do it here though. Housework, I mean. Since I'm not working and Rich is. But I don't like it. Anyway, Ingie's husband (he wasn't her husband yet at that point, of course) he had enough one day so he packed up and went home and got himself a Turkish wife who would do absolutely everything for him and then he brought her to this country where he could virtually lock her up while he made lots of money. We don't even know if he ever divorced his first wife. Ingie did not say any of this, of course. Just said he was a genius and loved his work and could fix any machine in the world and that his first wife is 'very bad girl' and that he is 'very happy, very joyful man'. And indeed, their Betamaxes are there to prove it. Him dancing in front of family and friends at Melody's third birthday. A film of him filming Melody and a pregnant Ingie romping in the woods on a holiday in Vermont. All very joyful. Ingie too is 'very joyful person'. When you visit her she always has some tape on – loud. Disco, rock, oriental music, whatever. And one of Melody's favourite games is to sit Wayne down, get her mother to put on some of that wailing, banging stuff, grab a scarf and start dancing for him. And she can dance. Arms and legs twirling. Neck side to side. Leaning backwards. The lot. And Wayne, who normally can't sit still for a minute, sits transfixed, watching a little blonde who cannot speak a word that means anything to him,

7

strutting and flirting about with a veil. I wasn't even sure this friendship was particularly good for him. But the tears and the tantrums that we had if I tried to stop him from going over – it was just easier to let him go. Once she was supposed to be coming to our apartment to play with him and she did not show. He just sat and waited. He wasn't even four yet but he sat and waited for her for over two hours and then he made me take him to Ingie's apartment and when they weren't there he sat down on the doorstep and wept. This whole compound, as far as he was concerned, was 'where Melody lives'. Melody didn't care as much as he did, I think. But then she had a little brother and Waynie has no one. Well, he has three brothers but they are much older and they're back in Vancouver. In point of fact, we too are a second family. Rich was married for fifteen years. I don't really know that much about his first wife – except he pays her a lot of alimony which is part of the reason why we're here. But he had three sons and he never wanted to have Wayne. Wayne was the result of a deal I made with Rich. When he got the offer of this job and he really wanted to take it, I said, 'OK. You give me what I want and you can have what you want.' I mean, not every woman would agree to be buried alive in a place like this, would she? So he signed the contract and we bought the jeep and set off overland and while we were crossing France I got myself pregnant. He joked a bit about making sure it was a girl, but after Wayne came he really chickened out and went and got himself vasectomised so I could

[handwritten marginalia: Wayne like a business deal]

not nag him for another kid. Ingie said that her husband was waiting for their third. Always talking about it. But Elaine said Ingie had told her she was on the Pill. She didn't want to get pregnant because some fortune-teller back home said that she would have three children and one would break her heart. So she figured if she only had two, that would somehow invalidate the whole prophecy. I don't know about all that. I mean, I don't believe in fortune-tellers myself but sometimes you hear stories of things they've said – well, anyway, Ingie's husband was on at her to have a third and every month he waited to see if she had conceived and meanwhile she's secretly on the Pill and hiding the strip among Melody's pants and vests and terrified that he should find out. That's what these Muslim men are like, they can never have enough children. Mostly though, they want boys. But this one wanted another girl. I asked Ingie how come he wanted a girl and she said he thought girls were more 'tender and loving' than boys. Besides, a boy would always end up 'belonging' to his wife while a girl was 'her father's daughter for ever'. 'But –' she added, 'of course we believe everything God bring is good.' Of course.

This was the kind of conversation you had with Ingie. She also knew everything about everything that happened, or – as was more often the case – that almost happened around the place: the children almost snatched, the near-rapes, the Filipinos almost executed but deported instead, the Germans who went crazy. For all her tartiness, though, she was a good mum.

9

They were both good parents and you always found them in Kiddiworld on the last Thursday of the month – Western Family Day – and there would be this massive grey-haired Turk, whizzing down the lighthouse slide with little Melody held tight on what Wayne called his 'lamp' while Ingie waved at them, clutching Murat to her breast and laughing.

Now, of course, you don't see them there any more. You don't see them anywhere, really. Even though they're still around. Well, nobody wants to see much of them to tell the truth. I mean, Elaine always said he was a bit weird but I never knew *how* weird until I heard all that stuff about the camera. But of course I didn't know that until later. When it happened I hadn't seen Ingie for a while. I'd actually stopped going round that much. I still took Wayne there. But I'd leave him then go and collect him. That night, though, I went. I had to. And the air in the compound was, as I said, not just full of the scent of jasmine, but literally heavy with it. It was eight o'clock and the older children were still out. Climbing the railings by the pool, running between the bushes, whispering, then a burst of laughter. I had to go. I knew that a lot of people had gone the night before and I'd watched people coming and going all morning and all afternoon. Well, that's maybe the Muslim way. But we usually just send a card. Or we go to the funeral. But I decided I'd better go or it would maybe look unfriendly. So I waited till I'd put Wayne to bed and I told Rich and I went out and it just hit me: how pleasant the night air was and how fragrant. I walked slowly because I had no idea what I should do or say once I got there and I looked up at their windows and they were all lit up and all the curtains wide open. I walked up the stairs and from outside the door I could hear the Qur'ān being chanted so I knocked and someone let me in and to the left were maybe twenty men sitting in a circle around a cassette player, silent. Screened from them, round the corner, huddled on the floor, a veiled woman, all in black, listened too. I stood unsure of what to do, then the woman got to her feet and it was Ingie. She opened the door to the inner bit of the apartment, let me in and closed the door behind us. She sat down on the sofa and I sat on a chair close to her. The apartment was full of women. Women and babies. Women sitting. Women making coffee. Women preparing food and handing it to the men outside. One woman was doing the dishes. Another was folding up some dry washing. All the women were in black. But the babies were bright spots of colour. Murat – in red dungarees and a red-and-white shirt – hung onto his mother's knees for a moment and then propelled himself towards his sister's shiny blue tricycle. He fell, cried, was picked up and dandled by one of the women. I finally looked full at Ingie. I was all ready to find that she had aged overnight. But she hadn't. She seemed, if anything, younger. She had lost a lot of weight. I don't know how she managed it in only twenty-three hours but she had and she looked slight and frail in her long black skirt and her black T-shirt. No make-up, her hair pulled back and knotted with a

rubber band, black circles around her eyes. Her skin –
not just the skin of her face but of her arms, hands and
feet, all you could see of her – had grown finer: almost
transparent. And she had lost her poise. Her movements were slow and awkward: adolescent. When she
sat, her feet turned inward, towards each other, like a
shy girl or a twisted doll. Her eyes were red and seeing
me look she pointed at them and whispered, 'I have no
tears.' She also had no voice. Even her whisper had to
be forced out. Every once in a while she would convulse
in what looked like the prelude to a fit of weeping but
then nothing would come of it and she would just sit
quiet again with a hand on each of her knees and feet
turned inward. Staring at her fingers she whispered,
'People live fifty years. Seventy years, even. She lived
fifty months.' The woman sitting next to her on the
sofa – a fat Egyptian who was perspiring so much you
couldn't tell the sweat from the tears – pointed at the
ceiling, then spread her hands, palms upward. Ingie
whispered, 'He gave her to me. Why He take her away?
Why?' The woman reached over and patted the hand
resting on the knee closer to her and said, 'You are a
Muslim.' Ingie's voice rattled as she struggled to break
out of her whisper. 'I am Muslim. But she was my
daughter.' Then she went into one of her brief, dry-
eyed convulsions. The woman patted her hand again
and turned and spoke in Arabic to her own daughter
hulking in black lace behind her. Ingie reached under a
cushion and took out a pack of blue Silk Cut. Three
Turkish women sprang up to get her an ashtray. After

two drags and a whole lot of coughing she stubbed it out. Her white arms – no bracelet, no rings other than her gold wedding-band – moved in dramatic gestures. 'I cannot believe. From yesterday I am thinking, she will come from here – she will run from there. I see her run. I still hear her cry "Mama!" A minute. All it is. One minute. I do it. *I* do it.' She hit her breast. The Turkish woman Elaine says is her best friend stepped in from the kitchen and stood for a minute watching her. The Egyptian woman grabbed her hand and said, 'But what happen? How it happen yesterday?'

'Yesterday,' Ingie whispers like a machine, a robot with batteries running low, 'yesterday we are at home all day. The children are restless. I take them to the shopping mall. My husband so tired, he not want to go. I say, "OK we walk." We take my friend downstairs and her baby. We go. We make the tour. We give the children ice-cream. We come back. Outside, I remember, no more *Cérélac* for Murat. I say to my friend, "You keep the children. I run across the road for *Cérélac*."' She looks around. 'I don't want to take Melody in the shop. She always want chocolates and sweets and I think is bad for her. My friend say, "OK". I cross. Then I hear Melody. "Mama!" I turn and she is run after me and the car came so fast . . .' There is silence. She shakes her head. 'I watching. He hit her then the car carry her long down the road then she fall and start to go over and over. Everyone – they are running and the man from Jasmine flower-shop he carry her and we run to hospital – but she is die.' Her hands fall on her knees and she looks around. Looks at me. Her eyes have a questioning, doubting look in them as though one of us might tell her she is wrong and Melody is not 'die'. The woman next to her murmurs in Arabic and two of the Turkish women – one with braids, round spectacles and a fat baby and the other very classy with perfectly painted nails and one of those serpent rings that cover a whole finger – have started to cry into some pink Kleenex. Ingie is rocking gently to and fro on the sofa while Murat leans against her legs and chews on a cucumber wedge. Melody's toys fill the room and a fat *Encyclopaedia of Home Medicine* lies on the desk in the corner.

A little later, when I leave, I linger in the garden. I don't really want to go home just yet and Rich is looking after Wayne for once so I go to Elaine's. I can't stay with her very long because it's evening and Mike – her husband – is there but I tell her about the scene at Ingie's and she says, 'He never goes out weekends. He works all week and sleeps all weekend. Kids get restless.' But, as I say, I did see him in Kiddiworld.

When I left Elaine I decided to go across the road and buy some flowers: a surprise for Rich because I don't often do that kind of thing – but just to say thank you for looking after Wayne.

I cross the road. There are no marks on the surface, no bent lamp-posts, no police cordon. Nothing to say that something out of the ordinary happened here last night.

The flower-man, a greasy Lebanese who I've never liked, said, 'You have seen what happened last night?'

'The child?'

'Ah!' he said. 'I saw it all. Nobody has a good view as me.'

I chose five red roses and he started to strip them of leaves and thorns.

'I am standing at the door here. I see the lady cross. I know her. Often I see her. Always with the children. This time I see her cross the road and the other lady wait with the children. Then, I see the little girl: she calls – and runs. The mother turns and the car just BOOM – ' He slams a fist into the open palm of his other hand – 'just BOOM and then carries her off: twenty-four metres. The mother is on the island in the middle of the road. Her arms are stretched out. But the screaming is from the brakes and the tyres.' He lays the roses carefully on a sheet of cellophane and bends to pick out some ferns to put with them.

'Me, I have started to run. The car drops her and she rolls over and over and she rolls into my arms like that. Blood is everywhere. I lift her. The head falls back and the eyes are all the way up so you can only see the white. But she is breathing. I hold her head against my chest and I run and run very fast to the hospital. The head, it is spurting blood at me – like a pump. Today, you know, I have asked my friend, the doctor – he plays chess with me – I have asked him how much blood is a child, just four, having in her body? He says maybe four litres. Well, I tell you: it was four litres on me and I don't know how much on the road. I did not even notice though, truly. I carried her to the hospital but she was dead. It was only later, when I have come back here, I start to smell. I look down and I am covered with blood.' He wrapped some aluminium foil carefully round the stems of the flowers to keep them moist.

I said, 'I heard her father rushed out and tried to kill the driver?'

'Ah! But they stopped him. What good would it do? He was speeding, yes. But they all speed, and he was not expecting a child to run into the middle of the road at ten o'clock at night. He is in prison now and he will pay compensation, you know: blood money.'

He tied a white ribbon round the cellophane-wrapped bouquet.

'He came here this morning with a video camera, the father. He was taking a film of the road. I went out to see and he made interview with me. He wanting me to do exactly like what happened. Here the car hit her, like this. Here, I pick her up, like this. I run like this. He took a whole film. Everything. The poor man.'

I gave him his money and went home with the roses. I put them in a vase and told Rich all about it but he had gotten into some book and I don't think he really wanted to hear. Elaine did, though. And I went to see her next morning as soon as I had put Waynie on the school bus. But all the while I was talking I had a feeling she was keeping something up her sleeve and sure enough when I'd finished she said, 'And you know what he did in the afternoon, the father? He went down to the morgue, where they were going to wash the poor child and lay her out, and he filmed the whole thing.'

'But how could they let him?'

'They said the poor man was so crazed with grief it was better to let him do whatever he wanted. Besides, they're afraid of him; he's a big guy – and violent. And do you know what he did in the evening after you'd left and all the others had gone and only Ingie's best friend was there?'

Elaine leaned forward with her arms on her knees.

'He sat Ingie down and made her watch both his films: the one on the road and the one in the morgue. And then he made her watch the film of Melody's last birthday. He said what happened is her fault and she has to be made to feel it.'

Well. That's weird. Weird enough for me anyway. They also say he wants her to get pregnant immediately and give him another daughter. And she is not allowed to take little Murat out at all because he can't trust her to look after him.

Melody was in the morgue for a week while they got her an exit visa and he got leave from his work and then they all flew out to Turkey to bury her in their home town. Elaine thinks that's morbid but I kind of understand they wouldn't want to leave the kid here on her own when they finally go away. They had a bad time of it though because it was that freak five days when all of Turkey and Jordan were covered in snow and the drive from the airport to their home town was ten hours. Still, I guess that was better than if it had been sweltering hot and all. Anyway. He blamed Ingie to everybody back home and she wanted to stay on with her mother a bit but he brought her back because he wasn't going to leave little Murat in her care and because she had to get pregnant. And now they're here and it's all a bit spooky. No one quite knows how to talk to them so we avoid them as much as we can. Everyone honestly thinks they ought to go away. But of course he's only done four years and he needs to do one more to qualify for the five-year bonus. We all understand that. But we don't understand her. How can she ever cross that road without thinking of Melody? How can she walk in the gardens? Live in the apartment?

That night I went to see her she suddenly leaned towards me and said, 'She was –' then she turned to the Turkish woman with the spectacles and asked something which appeared to be quite urgent. The Turkish woman looked serious and said, 'Good. Not selfish.'

'Yes,' said Ingie to me very earnestly. 'She was a good child. Not selfish. A good child.'

'I am sorry,' I said. 'So sorry.'

She stared at the carpet.

'She was my daughter. Now my house is empty.'

I patted her knee – the one the Egyptian woman wasn't patting.

'You have Murat.'

I left soon after that. Some women were leaving. Others were coming in. I didn't know it but Ingie's husband was fixing up his video shows. As I stepped out of the building the air seemed fresher and the scent of jasmine was even more strong. The children were still climbing the railings by the pool, buzzing with talk – and I remember wondering, how was I going to break the news to Waynie?

SANDPIPER

O utside, there is a path. A path of beaten white stone bordered by a white wall – low, but not low enough for me to see over it from here. White sands drift across the path. From my window, I used to see patterns in their drift. On my way to the beach, I would try to place my foot, just the ball of my foot, for there never was much room, on those white spaces that glinted flat and free of sand. I had an idea that the patterns on the stone should be made by nature alone; I did not want one grain of sand, blown by a breeze I could not feel, to change its course because of me. What point would there be in trying to decipher a pattern that I had caused? It was not easy. Balancing, the toes of one bare foot on the hot stone, looking for the next clear space to set the other foot down. It took a long time to reach the end of the path. And then the stretch of beach. And then the sea.

SANDPIPER

I used to sit where the water rolled in, rolled in, its frilled white edge nibbling at the sand, withdrawing to leave great damp half moons of a darker, more brownish-beige. I would sit inside one of these curves, at the very midpoint, fitting my body to its contour, and wait. The sea unceasingly shifts and stirs and sends out fingers, paws, tongues to probe the shore. Each wave coming in is different. It separates itself from the vast, moving blue, rises and surges forward with a low growl, lightening as it approaches to a pale green, then turns over to display the white frill that slides like a thousand snakes down upon itself, breaks and skitters up the sandbank. I used to sit very still. Sometimes the wave would barely touch my feet, sometimes it would swirl around me then pull back, sifting yet another layer of sand from under me, leaving me wet to the waist. My heels rested in twin hollows that filled, emptied and refilled without a break. And subtle as the shadow of a passing cloud, my half moon would slip down the bank – only to be overtaken and swamped by the next leap of foaming white.

I used to sit in the curve and dig my fingers into the grainy, compact sand and feel it grow wetter as my fingers went deeper and deeper till the next rippling, frothing rush of white came and smudged the edges of the little burrow I had made. Its walls collapsed and I removed my hand, covered in wet clay, soon to revert to dry grains that I would easily brush away.

I lean against the wall of my room and count: twelve years ago, I met him. Eight years ago, I married him. Six years ago, I gave birth to his child.

For eight summers we have been coming here; to the beach-house west of Alexandria. The first summer had not been a time of reflection; my occupation then had been to love my husband in this – to me – new and different place. To love him as he walked towards my parasol, shaking the water from his black hair, his feet sinking into the warm, hospitable sand. To love him as he carried his nephew on his shoulders into the sea, threw him in, caught him and hoisted him up again; a colossus bestriding the waves. To love him as he played backgammon with his father in the evening, the slam of counters and the clatter of dice resounding on the patio while, at the dining-room table, his sister showed me how to draw their ornate, circular script. To love this new him, who had been hinted at but never revealed when we lived in my northern land, and who after a long absence, had found his way back into the heart of his country, taking me along with him. We walked in the sunset along the water's edge, kicking at the spray, my sun-hat fallen on my back, my hand, pale bronze in his burnt brown, my face no doubt mirroring his: aglow with health and love; a young couple in a glitzy commercial for life insurance or a two-week break in the sun.

My second summer here was the sixth summer of our love – and the last of our happiness. Carrying my child and loving her father, I sat on the beach, dug holes in the sand and let my thoughts wander. I thought about our life in my country, before we were married: four years in the cosy flat, precarious on top of a roof in a Georgian square, him meeting me at the bus-stop when I came back from work, Sundays when it did not rain and we sat in the park with our newspapers, late nights at the movies. I thought of those things and missed them – but with no great sense of loss. It was as though they were all there, to be called upon, to be lived again whenever we wanted.

I looked out to sea and, now I realise, I was trying to work out my co-ordinates. I thought a lot about the water and the sand as I sat there watching them meet and flirt and touch. I tried to understand that I was on the edge, the very edge of Africa; that the vastness ahead was nothing compared to what lay behind me. But – even though I'd been there and seen for myself its never-ending dusty green interior, its mountains, the big sky, my mind could not grasp a world that was not present to my senses – I could see the beach, the waves, the blue beyond, and cradling them all, my baby.

I sat with my hand on my belly and waited for the tiny eruptions, the small flutterings, that told me how she lay and what she was feeling. Gradually, we came to talk to each other. She would curl into a tight ball in one corner of my body until, lopsided and uncomfortable, I coaxed and prodded her back into a more centred, relaxed position. I slowly rubbed one corner of my belly until *there*, aimed straight at my hand, I felt a gentle punch. I tapped and she punched again. I was twenty-nine. For seventeen years my body had waited to conceive, and now my heart and mind had caught up with it. Nature had worked admirably; I had wanted the child through my love for her father and how I loved her father that summer. My body could not get enough of him. His baby was snug inside me and I wanted him there too.

From where I stand now, all I can see is dry, solid white. The white glare, the white wall, and the white path, narrowing in the distance.

I should have gone. No longer a serrating thought but familiar and dull. I should have gone. On that swirl of amazed and wounded anger when, knowing him as I did, I first sensed that he was pulling away from me, I should have gone. I should have turned, picked up my child and gone.

I turn. The slatted blinds are closed against a glaring sun. They call the wooden blinds *sheesh* and tell me it's the Persian word for glass. So that which sits next to a thing is called by its name. I have had this thought many times and feel as though it should lead me somewhere; as though I should draw some conclusion from it, but so far I haven't.

I draw my finger along a wooden slat. Um Sabir, my husband's old nanny, does everything around the house, both here and in the city. I tried, at first, at least to help, but she would rush up and ease the duster or the vacuum cleaner from my hands. 'Shame, shame. What am I here for? Keep your hands nice and soft. Go and rest. Or why don't you go to the club? What have you to do with these things?' My husband translated all this for me and said things to her which I came to understand meant that tomorrow I would get used to their ways. The meals I planned never worked out. Um Sabir cooked what was best in the market on that day.

If I tried to do the shopping the prices trebled. I arranged the flowers, smoothed out the pleats in the curtains and presided over our dinner-parties.

My bed is made. My big bed which a half-asleep Lucy, creeping under the mosquito-net, tumbles into in the middle of every night. She fits herself into my body and I put my arm over her until she shakes it off. In her sleep she makes use of me; my breast is sometimes her pillow, my hip her footstool. I lie content, glad to be of use. I hold her foot in my hand and dread the time – so soon to come – when it will no longer be seemly to kiss the dimpled ankle.

On a black leather sofa in a transit lounge in an airport once, many years ago, I watched a Pakistani woman sleep. Her dress and trousers were a deep, yellow silk and on her dress bloomed luscious flowers in purple and green. Her arms were covered in gold bangles. She had gold in her ears, her left nostril and around her neck. Against her body her small son lay curled. One of his feet was between her knees, her nose was in his hair. All her worldly treasure was on that sofa with her, and so she slept soundly on. That image, too, I saved up for him.

I made my bed this morning. I spread my arms out wide and gathered in the soft, billowing mosquito-net. I twisted it round in a thick coil and tied it into a loose loop that dangles gracefully in mid-air.

Nine years ago, sitting under my first mosquito-net, I had written, 'Now I know how it feels to be a memsahib.' That was in Kano; deep, deep in the heart of the continent I now sit on the edge of. I had been in love with him for three years and being apart then was a variant, merely, of being together. When we were separated there was for each a gnawing lack of the other. We would say that this confirmed our true, essential union. We had parted at Heathrow, and we were to be rejoined in a fortnight, in Cairo, where I would meet his family for the first time.

I had thought to write a story about those two weeks; about my first trip into Africa: about Muhammad al-Senusi explaining courteously to me the inferior status of women, courteously because, being foreign, European, on a business trip, I was an honorary man. A story about travelling the long, straight road to Maiduguri and stopping at roadside shacks to chew on meat that I then swallowed in lumps while Senusi told me how the meat in Europe had no body and melted like rice pudding in his mouth. About the time when I saw the lion in the tall grass. I asked the driver to stop, jumped out of the car, aimed my camera and shot as the lion crouched. Back in the car, unfreezing himself from horror, the driver assured me that the lion had crouched in order to spring at me. I still have the photo: a lion crouching in tall grass – close up. I look at it and cannot make myself believe what could have happened.

I never wrote the story, although I still have the notes. Right here, in this leather portfolio which I take out of a drawer in my cupboard. My Africa story. I told it to him instead – and across the candlelit table of a Cairo restaurant he kissed my hands and said, 'I'm crazy about you.' Under the high windows the Nile flowed by. Eternity was in our lips, our eyes, our brows – I married him, and I was happy.

I leaf through my notes. Each one carries a comment, a description meant for him. All my thoughts were addressed to him. For his part he wrote that after I left him at the airport he turned round to hold me and tell me how desolate he felt. He could not believe I was not there to comfort him. He wrote about the sound of my voice on the telephone and the crease at the top of my arm that he said he loved to kiss.

What story can I write? I sit with my notes at my writing-table and wait for Lucy. I should have been sleeping. That is what they think I am doing. That is what we pretend I do: sleep away the hottest of the midday hours. Out there on the beach, by the pool, Lucy has no need of me. She has her father, her uncle, her two aunts, her five cousins; a wealth of playmates and protectors. And Um Sabir, sitting patient and watchful in her black *jalabiyyah* and *tarha*, the deck-chairs beside her loaded with towels, sun-cream, sun-hats, sandwiches and iced drinks in Thermos flasks.

I look, and watch, and wait for Lucy.

In the market in Kaduna the mottled, red carcasses lay on wooden stalls shaded by grey plastic canopies. At first I saw the meat and the flies swarming and settling. Then, on top of the grey plastic sheets, I saw the vultures. They perched as sparrows would in an English market square, but they were heavy and still and silent. They sat cool and unblinking as the fierce sun beat down on their bald, wrinkled heads. And hand in hand with the fear that swept over me was a realisation that fear was misplaced, that everybody else

knew they were there and still went about their
business; that in the meat-market in Kaduna, vultures
were commonplace.

The heat of the sun saturates the house; it seeps out
from every pore. I open the door of my room and walk
out into the silent hall. In the bathroom I stand in the
shower tray and turn the tap to let the cool water splash
over my feet. I tuck my skirt between my thighs and
bend to put my hands and wrists under the water. I press
wet palms to my face and picture grey slate roofs wet
with rain. I picture trees; trees that rustle in the wind
and when the rain has stopped, release fresh showers of
droplets from their leaves.

I pad out on wet feet that dry by the time I arrive at the
kitchen at the end of the long corridor. I open the fridge
and see the chunks of lamb marinading in a large metal
tray for tonight's barbecue. The mountain of yellow grapes
draining in a colander. I pick out a cluster and put it on a
white saucer. Um Sabir washes all the fruit and vegetables
in red permanganate. This is for my benefit since Lucy
crunches cucumbers and carrots straight out of the green-
grocer's baskets. But then she was born here. And now she
belongs. If I had taken her away then, when she was eight
months old, she would have belonged with me. I pour out
a tall glass of cold, bottled water and close the fridge.

I walk back through the corridor. Past Um Sabir's
room, his room, Lucy's room. Back in my room I stand
again at the window, looking out through the chink in
the shutters at the white that seems now to be losing
the intensity of its glare. If I were to move to the

31

window in the opposite wall I would see the green lawn encircled by the three wings of the house, the sprinkler at its centre ceaselessly twisting, twisting. I stand and press my forehead against the warm glass. I breathe on the window-pane but it does not mist over.

I turn on the fan. It blows my hair across my face and my notes across the bed. I kneel on the bed and gather them. The top one says, 'Ningi, his big teeth stained with Kola, sits grandly at his desk. By his right hand there is a bicycle bell which he rings to summon a gofer –', and then again: 'The three things we stop for on the road should be my title: "Peeing, Praying and Petrol".' Those were light-hearted times, when the jokes I made were not bitter.

I lie down on the bed. These four pillows are my innovation. Here they use one long pillow with two smaller ones on top of it. The bedlinen comes in sets. Consequently my bed always has two pillows in plain cases and two with embroidery to match the sheets. Also, I have one side of a chiffonier which is full of long, embroidered pillowcases. When I take them out and look at them I find their flowers, sheltered for so long in the dark, are unfaded, bright and new.

Lying on the bed, I hold the cluster of grapes above my face, and bite one off as Romans do in films. Oh, to play, to play again, but my only playmate now is Lucy and she is out by the pool with her cousins.

A few weeks ago, back in Cairo, Lucy looked up at the sky and said, 'I can see the place where we're going to be.'

'Where?' I asked, as we drove through Gabalaya Street.

'In heaven.'

'Oh!' I said. 'And what's it like?'

'It's a circle, Mama, and it has a chimney, and it will always be winter there.'

I reached over and patted her knee. 'Thank you, darling,' I said.

Yes, I am sick – but not just for home. I am sick for a time, a time that was and that I can never have again. A lover I had and can never have again.

I watched him vanish – well, not vanish, slip away, recede. He did not want to go. He did not go quietly. He asked me to hold him, but he couldn't tell me how. A fairy godmother, robbed for an instant of our belief in her magic, turns into a sad old woman, her wand into a useless stick. I suppose I should have seen it coming. My foreignness, which had been so charming, began to irritate him. My inability to remember names, to follow the minutiae of politics, my struggles with his language, my need to be protected from the sun, the mosquitoes, the salads, the drinking water. He was back home, and he needed someone he could be at home with, at home. It took perhaps a year. His heart was broken in two, mine was simply broken.

I never see my lover now. Sometimes, as he romps with Lucy on the beach, or bends over her grazed elbow, or sits across our long table from me at a dinner-party, I see a man I could yet fall in love with, and I turn away.

I told him too about my first mirage, the one I saw on that long road to Maiduguri. And on the desert road to Alexandria the first summer, I saw it again. 'It's hard to believe it isn't there when I can see it so clearly,' I complained.

'You only think you see it,' he said.

'Isn't that the same thing?' I asked. 'My brain tells me there's water there. Isn't that enough?'

'Yes,' he said, and shrugged. 'If all you want to do is sit in the car and see it. But if you want to go and put your hands in it and drink, then it isn't enough, surely?' He gave me a sidelong glance and smiled.

Soon, I should hear Lucy's high, clear voice, chattering to her father as they walk hand in hand up the gravel drive to the back door. Behind them will come the heavy tread of Um Sabir. I will go out smiling to meet them and he will deliver a wet, sandy Lucy into my care, and ask if I'm OK with a slightly anxious look. I will take Lucy into my bathroom while he goes into his. Later, when the rest of the family have all drifted back and showered and changed, everyone will sit around the barbecue and eat and drink and talk politics and crack jokes of hopeless, helpless irony and laugh. I should take up embroidery and start on those *Aubusson* tapestries we all, at the moment, imagine will be necessary for Lucy's trousseau.

Yesterday when I had dressed her after the shower she examined herself intently in my mirror and asked for a french plait. I sat behind her at the dressing-table blow-drying her black hair, brushing it and plaiting it. When Lucy was born Um Sabir covered all the mirrors. His sister said, 'They say if a baby looks in the mirror she will see her own grave.' We laughed but we did not remove the covers; they stayed in place till she was one.

I looked at Lucy's serious face in the mirror. I had seen my grave once, or thought I had. That was part of my Africa story. The plane out of Nigeria circled Cairo airport. Three times I heard the landing-gear come down, and three times it was raised again. Sitting next to me were two Finnish businessmen. When the announcement came that we were re-routeing to Luxor they shook their heads and ordered another drink. At dawn, above Luxor airport, we were told there was trouble with the undercarriage and that the pilot was going to attempt a crash-landing. I thought, so this is why they've sent us to Luxor, to burn up discreetly and not clog Cairo airport. We were asked to fasten our seat belts, take off our shoes and watches, put the cushions from the backs of our seats on our laps and bend double over them with our arms around our heads. I slung my handbag with my passport, tickets and money around my neck and shoulder before I did these things. My Finnish neighbours formally shook each other's hands. On the plane there was perfect silence as we dropped out of the sky. And then a terrible, agonised, protracted screeching of machinery as we hit the Tarmac. And in that moment, not only my head, but all of me, my whole being, seemed to tilt into a blank, an empty radiance, but lucid. Then three giant thoughts. One was of him – his name, over and over again. The other was of the children I would never have. The third was that the pattern was now complete: this is what my life amounted to.

When we did not die, that first thought: his name, his name, his name became a talisman, for in extremity, hadn't all that was not him been wiped out of my life? My life, which once again stretched out before me, shimmering with possibilities, was meant to merge with his.

I finished the french plait and Lucy chose a blue clasp to secure its end. Before I let her run out I smoothed some after-sun on her face. Her skin is nut-brown, except just next to her ears where it fades to a pale cream gleaming with golden down. I put my lips to her neck. 'My Lucy, Lucia, *Lambah*,' I murmured as I kissed her and let her go. Lucy. My treasure, my trap.

Now, when I walk to the sea, to the edge of this continent where I live, where I almost died, where I wait for my daughter to grow away from me, I see different things from those I saw that summer six years ago. The last of the foam is swallowed bubbling into the sand, to sink down and rejoin the sea at an invisible subterranean level. With each ebb of green water the sand loses part of itself to the sea, with each flow another part is flung back to be reclaimed once again by the beach. That narrow stretch of sand knows nothing in the world better than it does the white waves that whip it, caress it, collapse onto it, vanish into it. The white foam knows nothing better than those sands which wait for it, rise to it and suck it in. But what do the waves know of the massed, hot, still sands of the desert just twenty, no, ten feet beyond the scalloped edge? And what does the beach know of the depths, the cold, the currents just there, there – do you see it? – where the water turns a deeper blue.

CHEZ MILOU

M ilou sits behind the cash desk. There is a grey checked rug on her knees and on the rug sits Athène. Athène is a comfortable dachshund the colour of expensive leather. She is sleek and plump but there's no doubt that she is growing old; you can see it in her eyes. Occasionally she ventures on to the floor and pauses briefly amidst the feet of the waiters. But then Milou gets anxious and leans over to look and call for her and Athène hurries back. She has to be helped on to her mistress's knee by one of the waiters – usually old Sayim, the Nubian. All day long Milou cuddles Athène. Milou's manicured fingers have thickened but she still wears her grandmother's heavy Russian rings. Her hands are mottled with liver-spots and they are uncertain on the cash register. They are heavy on Athène's back; stroking her smooth length, fondling the drooping ears or scratching the worried brow as the old dog whimpers quietly.

Milou might have married Philippe, but that was long ago. Now, all day Milou watches the frayed red velvet curtains screening the entrance to the restaurant. She knows all her customers, though she never smiles and only nods sternly to the oldest and the most regular. The young tourists who stray in and park their backpacks by the door puzzle over this large, grim woman with the red hennaed hair, who never leaves her seat. Yet despite the slight frown that Milou's features settle into when her thoughts wander, her customers find her a benign presence – and they come back.

To her left, and slightly to her rear, so that she cannot see him unless she turns around, old Monsieur Vasilakis sits in a corner of the restaurant. He sits at a round table with a small black-and-white television flickering soundlessly on a cutlery cabinet in front of him and a carafe of red wine always at his elbow. Monsieur Vasilakis is nearing ninety and almost all the friends who used to occupy the other chair at his table, share his wine and stare companionably at his flickering TV, have passed away. Milou usually knows exactly what he is doing even though her gaze is fixed in front of her. Today, it is Monsieur Vasilakis who is aware of his daughter's corner; the cash desk has been extended by a table with a white cloth, and a chair has been placed beside Milou's.

Milou observes the red curtains with particular

purpose; she is expecting a friend. Well, Farah is too young to be quite a friend; it is her mother, Latifa, really who is Milou's friend and, since their friendship dates from Latifa's wedding-night, Milou has known Farah since she was born. Latifa's wedding-night. Milou does not actually shudder or indeed feel anything much at all. But she remembers. She remembers the shame and the misery which for years that phrase had evoked in her; the shiver moving up her back, into her shoulders and arms until her fingers tingled with it, the cold weight in her stomach that she had had to rub and press into something she could bear. Latifa's wedding-night: when Milou had fled down the dark servants' staircase into Ismail Morsi's apartment to find his daughter, the bride, in the bathroom pulling off her veil and demolishing the elaborate chignon her hair had been pinned into. 'I hate this,' Latifa was muttering into the mirror, 'and so does he. We'll wear the stupid clothes and sit on the platform to be stared at like monkeys but I don't feel like *me* with this thing on my head and I am not having it –' Then she had turned and seen Milou. She drew her in and bolted the door. She sat her down on the edge of the bathtub and made her drink some water and Milou told her everything. How strange that then it had seemed that she must die; that tomorrow could not happen. And now it was as though the whole thing were a film she had seen. A film which had moved her for a while.

Milou had first seen Philippe amid the ululations and the clash of cymbals at a friend's wedding in the Greek

Orthodox Cathedral on Shari el-Malika Street. Milou
was twenty then. She was tall and well-built and
handsome. Her father, Khawaga Vasilakis, sitting over
his wine after their last customer had gone – watching
her as she strode through the darkened restaurant
folding up white tablecloths to take home for Faheema
to wash – her father would often tell her then that she
had her mother's shapely legs and her exuberant
auburn hair. He always made this observation sadly.
Then he would shake his head and bite the ends of his
drooping grey moustache as he stared into his glass.
Milou knew that her mother was French, had been a
dancer and had been beautiful – maybe still was. She
had abandoned her husband and the one-year-old
Milou for – of all things – a Turkish soldier: a black-
eyed, whiskered brigand who had swaggered off his
ship and into the Allied restaurant in Alexandria one
fine day in 1927 to wreck Theo Vasilakis's life. After
three years of alternately swearing to smash the whore's
face if she dared show it in the Allied and vowing that
everything would be forgiven if only she would come
back, for after all she was the mother of his child, Theo
could bear Alexandria no longer. He sold the restaurant and took Milou and Faheema, the black maid who
looked after them, to Cairo. He never saw his wife
again and he withstood all pressure to remarry. He
opened Chez Milou (instantly 'Shameelu' to the locals)
on the rue Abd-el-Khaleq Sarwat, and looked forward
to the day when his daughter would be a partner and
an adornment in the restaurant. Now that Milou was

both, her father watched her constantly and lived in terror of the swashbuckler who would come to lure her away and ruin her father's patched-up life for the second and final time. For a swashbuckler it would have to be. You only had to look at the girl – the long, strong legs, the lean waist, the straight back, the broad forehead, wide-set eyes and brilliant hair – to see the swarthy, muscled, sweating, tobacco-spitting son-of-a-bitch who would claim her. Khawaga Vasilakis's paunch trembled with apprehension and distaste and he chewed on his moustache.

But Milou saw Philippe amid the incense and the burning candles in the Greek Orthodox Cathedral and thought he looked like an angel: the boy – he could hardly be called a man – was so fair and so still. He sat at the far end of the pew on the other side of the aisle; the bridegroom's side. He was so separate that he appeared to belong more to the shining Byzantine icons on the walls than to the mass of breathing, moving people around him. Milou could see only his head in a three-quarter profile. His face was pale and fine-featured. Gleaming black hair rose smoothly from a white brow. His nose was chiselled. His mouth wide, his lips narrow and ascetic. She could not make out the colour of his unmoving eyes. But it was a quality of serenity, a combination of his utter stillness and the way his head shone like an illumination in the dim cathedral that so captured Milou.

Having no mother to do this work for her, Milou managed to find out who he was and – despite her dismay at confirming that he was indeed only seventeen and still at school with the Jesuit *frères* – she contrived an introduction. Milou found that Philippe stood a few centimetres taller than herself. She found that his eyes were green-grey and that his voice was mellow. His French was chic, more chic than her own, and his Arabic more broken. She found that even close up his skin kept its luminous quality. She imagined that there was something extraordinary – extramortal almost – about him, and longed to reach out and touch his face just on that fragile, contoured cheek-bone and rest her fingertips in the shallow dips at the outer corners of his black-fringed eyes. She found out that he was the son of Yanni Panayotis, the grocer, and therefore that he was a neighbour of one of her father's oldest friends, Ismail Morsi, who owned a furniture shop in the market in Ataba Square.

Philippe bowed his head slightly, as though the better to hear anything she might say. He smiled, and his eyes said that something amazing had happened. Milou surprised herself; she had never before felt this rushing frailty, this tremulous energy, and it never occurred to her to wonder whether he had felt it too.

The year was 1946 and the victorious Allied soldiers were everywhere in the city. Khawaga Vasilakis thought his daughter showed remarkable acumen when she announced that since their business was doing well, it was foolish to go on buying provisions piecemeal from the neighbouring shops; from now on, she declared, she would buy what they needed once a week, wholesale, from the market.

Yanni Panayotis's grocery was on the very outer fringe of the market – almost, in fact, in Shari el-Khaleeg, that wide road which until so recently would turn into a river in the season of the flood. Milou had never been that far from rue Sarwat before and the first time she went, Faheema, who knew all the roads and the alleys of the city, went with her. They walked down King Fouad Street and stared in the windows of the *grands magasins*, then crossed Opera Square, through the very tip of the notorious Azbakiyyah district, across the busy swirl of Ataba Square and into the teeming, narrow Mouski. Faheema started to point out grocers' shops in the alleys along the way but Milou would have none of them. It had to be Yanni Panayotis's store they went to and his was the furthest one of all. Faheema, who was neither young nor green, and whose breath was getting shorter as she hurried to keep up with her striding charge, began to grow suspicious. What would a grocery store have that would make a normally reasonable girl march ardently to the end of the world for it like this? There was only one answer possible. Faheema pursed her lips, collected her *melayah* round her and puffed after Milou.

Yanni Panayotis was a big man with a great deal of shaggy black hair streaked with silver. He made up for his broadening forehead by growing a wild beard and moustache. He liked the looks of both women and sat them down in his dark, cool shop and offered them tea and chocolates. From then on, Milou always went to Shari el-Khaleeg on Sunday. She went one week and then the next and the third time he was there. He was helping his father stack a delivery of large tins of white cheese and Milou sipped at her scalding tea and watched his broad back move under the fine white cotton shirt as he bent and straightened and lifted and reached. She glanced at the grey linen trousers shaping themselves around him as he squatted down in front of the cheese, but then she bit her lip and kept her eyes on the sawdust-strewn floor. When he had finished, Philippe took out a pressed white handkerchief from his pocket and wiped his brow. He was formal as he declined his father's offer of a cold drink. 'I will leave you to conduct your business.' He bowed over Milou's hand. '*Enchanté*, Mam-selle, a most happy opportunity.' He smiled into her eyes, and left. Yanni turned to Milou, shrugging and spreading his hands wide, and saw at once her passion for his son in the girl's high colour and rigid posture. Ah. So that's it, he thought. It is for this that it is Sunday, and always Sunday; the little Philippe has lit a fire –

'And what a fire that will be,' he commented to his wife that night. 'The girl is beautiful and her hair is in flames already.' Nina turned down the corners of her mouth and pouted at the husband who, after two married daughters and a son who could, if he wished, grow whiskers and a beard, could still sweet-talk her back into bed with him on a Monday morning when the shop was closed and the boy had gone to school and Nina was in her flowered silk dressing-gown, belted to show off her still-tiny waist. She would glance up at the mahogany display cabinet hanging in the corner above their bed with her bridal veil and its crown of orange-blossom inside it and remonstrate that it was unseemly to behave like a honeymoon couple and draw the blinds in the morning after twenty-five years of marriage and what would the neighbours think? Khawaga Yanni grunted affectionately as he nuzzled his moustache into his wife's neck. 'They will say, the old fool is still crazy for her – and they will be right, no? Is that not so, little one? Ah, my little one –' And Nina would hold him gently and let him love her and think what a wonderful stew she would make for his lunch. Now she pouted and stared down at the *petit point* in her hand: the girl is too old; she is four years older than Philippe. Yanni should not be easygoing on such matters. A man can tire easily of a wife older than himself. Of course, on the other hand she has no mother or brother to make trouble and when Monsieur Vasilakis – God grant him long life – goes, she will be the sole owner of a restaurant in a very good part of town.

The discussions continued and Milou's visits to the shop continued. Philippe left the *frères* and joined the Faculty of Commerce and still every Sunday morning Milou would walk across town to the grocery store in Shari el-Khaleeg, take tea with Khawaga Panayotis, and hire a *calèche* to carry her and her provisions back to the rue Sarwat. Sometimes she began to despair, to lose heart – but then she would see him, and each time she was freshly convinced that he had 'intentions'; their glance had met for a fraction longer, his smile had asked a question – a question she longed to answer. Until Latifa's wedding-night.

Days before, Faheema, on the floor at Milou's feet with her mouth full of pins and her hands full of shiny, emerald green taffeta, Faheema had urged her to make a move. 'You either get him out of your head or you sort him out. A woman has to manage, you know. Three years have passed and it's, "I'm sure I felt him press my hand," "today he actually touched it with his lips" – what is this stupid talk? Is this child's play, or what? Maybe he's still young and doesn't understand how things work. Or maybe he has nothing for women. Some of your men are like that, you Greeks. Except – look at his father: there's a man for you, a man who fills his clothes. But you are not going to spend your whole life waiting. He doesn't speak? You've got a tongue. Make a little skirmish. See what clay he's formed of –'

To get to the roof-terrace where the wedding party was being held, guests had to go through Ismail Morsi's flat, out of its back door and up the wrought iron, unlit servants' staircase. The stairs had been freshly washed for the occasion and gleamed bright black in the darkness. The rubbish pails that normally stood on the landings had been kept indoors and the cats – who lived off the rubbish – stayed away. The large terrace was hung with lights and a marquee at one end provided a multicoloured backdrop for the bridal dais. The drums beat out and the accordions wailed for all the neighbourhood to hear and the hired, white-robed *sofragis* circled with silver trays of sherbet and chocolates and almond-filled sweets. Milou excused herself from the bride's younger sister Soraya, and slipped away. Later, she tried to determine what had made her choose that particular moment – but she never could. She just remembered how she had leaned over and whispered a few words to Soraya, then, exchanging a look with Faheema, cross-legged with the other women servants on the carpet at the foot of the bridal bower, she had picked the skirt of her gown off the floor and headed for the stairs.

Milou turned a corner of the staircase and saw a man climbing out of the dark towards her. She stood still as Philippe, unaware, continued up the stairs. Then, he must have heard a rustle, or perhaps he felt her breath, for he stopped. He looked up – and there it came again: the smile that barely touched his lips but shone through his eyes.

'*Bonsoir!*'

Never before, and never again did Milou look as radiant as she did then: gathering her softly rustling dress, bare arms white against the green tulle of the bodice, her '*bonsoir*' was the merest whisper. Philippe stood to one side to let her pass, for of course he knew that it would be most improper to linger on the stairs. Milou lifted her skirt and stepped slowly down. The music pulsed down the stairwell. Milou drew level with Philippe. She turned as though to pass him sideways because of the narrowness of the stairs – and then she stopped. She was so close that she felt her breasts brush against him and her skirt fall around his legs. Milou lifted her face and his eyes looked into hers. She whispered his name and her hand let go of the crushed taffeta and rose to rest lightly against his cheek. Now, now he must surely – but Philippe, too well-bred to step back, merely stood unmoving and Milou's hand drew away, went to her face, her throat, then clutched at the skirt again as she whirled around, ran down the stairs and into the bathroom where Latifa was tugging the grips out of her hair.

Milou frowned at the red curtain which was opening to admit a very pretty young woman in a short-sleeved white cotton dress. She wore her sun-glasses pushed to the top of her head and holding back her dark shoulder-length hair.

'*Chérie!*' cried Milou, and held up her hands. Athène woke up and growled deep in her throat.

'Tante Milou!' Farah said, bending to hug Milou's shoulders and kiss her on both cheeks. Farah sat on the chair next to Milou, asked a passing waiter for some iced water, fanned herself with a magazine, tickled Athène's ears and began the ritual complaint about parking and the heat. 'I've parked at the Opera and walked all the way up. But it is absolutely the only place and I'm going to see Tante Soraya later so I guess it makes sense.'

'She is still in your grandfather's old flat – God have mercy on him?'

'Oh, yes. She's still in Ataba. That's one thing that doesn't change, thank goodness. It's exactly the same as when my grandfather was alive. Even his bed is still there. Oh –' remembering, 'Shall I go and say hello to Monsieur Vasilakis? Or will I disturb him?'

'Don't bother,' said Milou. 'He won't know you anyway. He's become even more vague since Faheema died. He was used to her.'

'God grant him long life.'

'Ah, well. He is certainly granting him that,' Milou nodded.

'But . . . things must be difficult for you, Tante Milou?' Farah said uncertainly.

Milou was silent, considering her fingers on Athène's back. She was not smiling. Farah stood up.

'I'm going to go and greet him.'

Milou did not look around as her guest bent over the old man and said his name gently. Watery, red-rimmed eyes shifted from the still life of flowers on the television and looked up.

'I'm Farah, M'sieur. Do you remember me?'

Theo Vasilakis nodded several times and returned to the screen. Farah laid a tentative hand on his shoulder.

'They haven't changed this picture for three days,' he complained. 'Between every two programmes this is what we get. They do have other tableaux: some with trees and some with birds; swans, you know.' His hand moved in the air, wavering. 'But they've been using *this* for three days. People can get bored. Eh. Well . . .' He watched the flowers resignedly. Sayim, the Nubian, paused.

'It's all right, Sitt Farah,' he said gently. 'The khawaga is fine. You go and sit with Sitt Milou. See what you would like for lunch. The *fatta* is very good today –'

'I'm going to eat *fatta*, 'Am Sayim?'

'Yes, why not? Don't talk to me about a *régime*; you're as thin as a stick. You could do with some flesh on you. Go and sit and I'll get you a good lunch. Leave it to me.'

Farah went back to her chair. Athène was asleep again, or at least her eyes were closed. Milou looked up and smiled.

'So. Tell me, *chérie*, how is Maman?'

'She's all right,' Farah shrugged. 'I guess she's happy where she is; away from us all.'

'*C'est dommage ça*; her staying away like this. And it can't make things easier for you? Especially now?'

'No. Sometimes I'd like to talk to her. And it's harder living with my father when she's not there. Although I suppose in a way it isn't really since they were getting on so badly – I don't know. Tante Soraya helps a lot, though – with the practical things; like looking after Adam for me. And I go and stay with her sometimes – for a break from being with my father. I feel much more comfortable at my grandfather's – at her place, really. You know, having grown up there and all that. But I can't really talk to her –'

'She dotes on you. You've always been her child –'

'But she's so bitter now. And sort of – hard. She's always irritated with uncle – her husband. And she's completely disappointed in her son and tells him so – all the time. She keeps pressuring me to go back to "Adam's father" and when I say we were unhappy together she looks at me like I'm mad and says, "So what? Who's happy in this world?"'

'Your mother seems happy –'

'Yes, but *she's* doing it all the wrong way round; discovering freedom and the pleasures of living alone now, after a million years of marriage. Still, she has a right. She says she reads in bed and she sleeps with the window open and she doesn't bother to cook but eats cheese and salads and fruit –' Farah giggled.

'And Papa? He is not unhappy?'

'Oh no. He's not bothered. I mean – I suppose he'd have preferred it if she'd stayed around and gone on being exactly as he wanted her to be. But since she started, you know, speaking up for herself, I guess he thinks he's better off on his own. You can't really tell with him, though –'

'Aren't you going to have any lunch or what?'

Farah got to her feet. Monsieur Vasilakis was standing next to her.

'Well? Aren't you going to offer your friend something to eat?' The voice was querulous.

Farah glanced at Milou and answered quickly. ''Am Sayim is bringing me some lunch in a minute. Won't you join us, Monsieur?'

'He's no use any more, the old idiot. He's gone senile.' Vasilakis was glancing around him as he muttered.

Farah brought over a chair from the nearest table. 'There you are, Monsieur Vasilakis. Please sit with us.'

Now she was between the old man and his daughter.

'Where is the food for your guest?'

Farah glanced at Milou's set face and unease built up inside her; an old familiar unease. For years she had heard her grandfather use this tone to the daughter who had elected to stay and look after him. For years she had watched Tante Soraya's face set in just such a closed look as this one. The waiter appeared with a tray.

'That's the spirit, Khawaga!' he beamed. 'You join the ladies and give the telly a rest. There's nothing on it but empty talk anyway, *and* it's all repeated.' He set the dishes down in front of Farah. 'I'll go get the khawaga's wine. Have a glass of wine, Sitt Milou, with the khawaga,' he urged.

Milou shook her head. The carafe and one half-full glass were placed on the table. 'Eat in good health and happiness,' Sayim smiled at Farah. 'You bring good company to us and light up our restaurant.'

'And what about you?' Milou stroked Athène and continued as though there had been no interruption. 'What about you, *ma petite*? Are you better off on your own too?'

'Oh, Tante Milou,' sighed Farah, poking at the stuffed courgettes. 'It's so difficult being a divorced woman here. I didn't think it would be this difficult.'

'It's just because you haven't got your own flat.' Milou lifted a hand from Athène and reached over to pat Farah. 'When you have your own flat it will all be different.'

'But I'm never going to have my own flat.' Farah put down her fork.

'You've already bought a flat –'

'Yes, but the man hasn't even started building it yet. It's all on paper. If he starts *tomorrow* it won't take him less than five years and I'm practically thirty already. I really never thought it would be so difficult.'

'Everything is difficult now. Everything,' said Monsieur Vasilakis. He put down his glass and leaned forward, a hand on each knee. 'Everything's changed. Life has become difficult. Very difficult.' He shook his head. 'In old times, it took fourteen different types of fish to make a bouillabaisse. I used to pick each fish personally. Nowadays what can you find? Three – four types maybe. Impossible to make a *vraie* bouillabaisse. Your father, he understood these things, he would tell me from the night before: Khawaga Theo, tomorrow we eat bouillabaisse –'

'Papa, do you know who this is?'

'Eh? Of course I know who this is. Ismail Morsi's daughter –'

'Ismail Morsi's daughter's daughter, Papa.' Milou's voice was flat.

'I know, I know.' The old man was impatient. 'You've always been friends together, you two. Even though she married and you didn't.' He turned to Farah. 'Your daughter must be *une belle demoiselle* by now, eh?'

'Farah has a boy, Papa. His name is Adam. He's almost nine?' turning to Farah.

'Almost. And he's utterly gorgeous. I would have brought him with me but he's spending the day with his cousins. He's my whole life now, Tante Milou. I don't know what I'd have done if he wasn't with me. I can't imagine how some people go through life without ever – oh, Tante Milou. I'm sorry –'

'It's all right, *chérie*,' Milou patted Athène and scratched the dog's neck. 'Don't worry. That's all in the past now. But what about – *il y'a quelq'un? Un homme?*'

'Man, what man?' Monsieur Vasilakis had turned to see what was happening on television, but now he turned back, suspicious. 'Aren't you married, child? My daughter herself went to your wedding –'

Farah touched Milou's arm gently. 'I am divorced, Monsieur. My husband and I have left each other.'

'Divorced, divorced, that is all one hears nowadays. Nobody has patience any more.' Monsieur Vasilakis sorrowed. 'It wasn't so in our day. You waited. Maybe one partner makes a mistake. The other one waits. If one pulls a bit, the other lets go a bit. That way the world can go on. Life wants patience. Eh . . . so you're divorced? A waste of the money your father spent on your wedding. He had a big wedding for you, I know. Milou was there. A man who knew how to do things, your father: a proper man.'

When her father had been silent for a few moments, sucking on the ends of his moustache and shaking his head sadly, Milou repeated quietly, 'So, my dear. What about a man?'

Monsieur Vasilakis came to again. 'Stay away from men.' He looked earnestly at Farah. 'Sons of bitches all of them. They have form and look impressive and inside they're worm-eaten. Leave them alone. Especially now. There *used* to be men. Why the King himself used to dine here. And Eden. He ate at that table over there – with Montgomery. Anthony Eden, you know?' He nodded. Then he turned slowly in his chair to the television.

'I'm not interested, Tante Milou. No, truly. The few – two men in fact – that I sort of *could* like are already married, firmly married. Other than that, I've had one proposal and you should have heard it: "As for the fact of you being a divorcee, I am prepared to overlook it –" And he was supposed to be "progressive". No. And besides, I don't want any conflicts around Adam. There was – ' Farah paused. 'I did think of an "arrangement" –'

'An "arrangement"?'

'A "marriage of convenience," I suppose it's called. I'm fed up with all the emotional stuff and I know I'm not going to be in love again; I don't want to be. But I do need a set-up, I need somewhere to live –'

'What are you talking about? This is a theory? Or there is a real person somewhere you are thinking of?'

'Oh I'm not really thinking about it any more. But yes. There is someone. But it's really too ridiculous.'

'Is it someone from the club? An old friend from school? What is ridiculous?'

'Oh, no, no, nothing like that. It's a neighbour – of Tante Soraya's. You might even know him –'

Milou stared at Farah.

'Do you know him, Tante Milou? Monsieur Philippe? Panayotis? Tante Milou?'

'No. No, not really.'

'Well, they've been Tante Soraya's neighbours for ever. He's really quite old, I suppose. I don't know exactly *how* old. He doesn't look too bad though – and he has a very gentle manner. Adam likes him. But I must say the main thing that made me think was the flat. They are magnificent those flats, Tante Milou, aren't they? The high ceilings, the cornices, the long corridors. And *his* flat has even got some amazing pre-war wallpaper which looks as though it was put up yesterday. And then of course there's all that marvellous old furniture that his mother had when she was a bride absolutely light years ago. Imagine. But I know it's wrong to think like that and anyway there's something kind of spooky about it all – how come you've never met him, Tante Milou?'

'I have – met him. At occasions: weddings and so. That's all.'

'Well, there is only him and Nina – that's his mother. He has sisters but they've been settled in Greece for ever and his father has been dead a long time. But Monsieur Philippe still lives with Nina. It's quite strange really, when you think of it, because Tante

Soraya says that he's always had the same job since he graduated; some small accountancy job. She won't really talk about him though – just says, "Philippe never changes" and that's the end of it. But she did tell me that he wouldn't take over his father's business when old Monsieur Yanni died –'

'Yanni, eh? old Yanni the grocer?' Monsieur Vasilakis only half-turned around. 'He was a good man too, God have mercy on him, like your father. We didn't see much of him here, but Milou used to buy all our groceries from him. Every week. He had a shop at the very end of the Mouski. Every week she would go there and come back with the groceries in a *calèche*. He gave her good discounts; for old customers, you know Greeks together. His daughters went back to Athens, but he had a son, too. A beautiful boy, they said, *and* he went to university. But we don't know anything about him –'

'Didn't you like the *fatta*, then, Sitt Farah?' Sayim was disappointed at the pile of bread and rice left on the plate.

'It was delicious, 'Am Sayim, but I could never finish it. I'm afraid I picked out all the meat, though.'

'This won't do, Sitt Farah. This won't do –'

'And I've eaten up all my vegetables.' Farah smiled up at the old waiter removing the plates.

Milou looked at Farah: 'When you say you considered marrying – this man, he has asked you?'

'Oh I'm not going to marry him, Tante Milou! I was just, you know, playing with the idea.'

'But has he asked you?' Athène stood up and tried to get off her mistress's knee but Milou held her by the collar.

'Oh no.'

'Well then?'

'But he would if I wanted him to.'

'But he is Christian, Orthodox?'

'He would become Muslim.'

'But how do you know? How do you know he would?'

'Tante Milou. One knows these things. There's definitely something in his eyes when he looks at me, and when I meet him on the stairs or he comes home from work and finds me chatting to Nina he always looks as though something terrific has happened. I don't talk to Tante Soraya about this kind of thing but Nadia, my youngest aunt, noticed and said she thought Monsieur Philippe had a *tendresse* for me.'

'Nadia? Now she's really your father's darling, isn't she?'

Monsieur Vasilakis was animated. 'He would bring her in here when she was only so high and sit her properly at the table and let her order whatever she wanted! Ah! What a world! The last of the bunch is always pure sugar as they say. How would I know? I only had Milou.' Monsieur Vasilakis drooped again. He put out a shaky hand for his glass. 'She was everything to me. Everything.'

Milou held on to Athène's collar. 'Tell me,' she said, straightening up, 'tell me. If you thought a man had a *tendresse* for you, but he wasn't doing anything about it. And you wanted to hurry him up a little so you made a move, an unmistakable move; one that nobody could pretend had been a misunderstanding. And he – he ignored it – ignored you. What would you feel?'

'It can't happen,' answered Farah firmly.

'But if it did?'

'It can't happen. But if it did, then – I suppose I shouldn't care for him after that. But it is a lovely word, isn't it, Tante Milou?'

'What? What is?'

'*Tendresse.*'

'Ah,' said Milou. '*Tendresse* . . . of course.'

THE WATER-HEATER

The flat was silent except for the steady hiss of the water-heater; a sound he was not completely used to yet. Until two months ago whenever he had wanted to have a bath the primus had to be lit. Faten had always lit it for him.

Every afternoon, when he woke from his siesta, he would knock at the door of his mother's room. Her voice, faint, would float out from within. 'Come in, my son.'

He would enter the darkened room to find her sitting up in the big brass bed, her head bound up in a white kerchief, a braid of still-black hair falling over one shoulder.

'Sit down, my son.' And he would seat himself on one of the two wooden *Assiuti* armchairs, under the window, to the right of the bed.

'How are you today, Mother?'

She always sighed before she answered: 'Thanks be to God . . . What can we say?'

In a while, she would ask: 'How is university, my son?' And he always answered: 'Thanks be to God, it is well.'

Some minutes would pass in silence, then the weak voice would call out, 'Faten, make some tea for Salah.'

Faten would bring the tea in small gold-rimmed glasses on a round silver tray, engraved with an image of the Holy House in Makkah. She would offer it first to her mother and then to her brother. She would place the tray on the round table by the bed and turn to him. 'Shall I heat the water for your bath now?'

He would nod. He would hear her lighting the primus, filling the large aluminium urn, and balancing it on the fire. She would check it every once in a while till at last she would come to the door. 'The water's ready for your bath.' Then she would turn away. She always spoke softly, and she always turned away.

Later, cleansed from the day's dust and from the sweat and mysterious impurities of sleep, he would put on a fresh white *jalabiyyah* and cap and perform the sunset prayers. Then he would sit cross-legged on the tiny Istanbul sofa on his balcony, telling his prayer-beads or reciting the Qur'ān till the time came for evening prayers.

He passed the prayer-beads absently through his fingers, his mind automatically recounting the ninety-nine names of God, his lips whispering them: 'the

Compassionate, the Merciful, the King, the Sacred, the Peaceful, the Believer . . .'

This evening his routine had been broken. He had not taken tea with his mother. She was not at home; she had gone to grieve with a friend who had just lost her husband. He had gone to the funeral yesterday but his mother would go every day for three days, then every Thursday for three Thursdays, then on the fortieth day, then on every anniversary. Although almost invalided by his father's death four months before, she still performed her social duties – the ones to do with death more avidly perhaps than others.

But the routine had been broken in another, more important way. He had not performed the sunset prayers. In fact he had not performed any of the day's prayers.

Salah raised his eyes. From where he sat he could see – through the open door of his room and across the narrow hallway with its dining-table and chairs – the bathroom door. The glass panel above the door showed that the room was filled with steam. And he could hear the hiss of the water-heater. He averted his eyes and tried to concentrate on the prayer-beads. 'Most powerful God, I return to Thee and beg Thy forgiveness . . .'

He was an 'ideal'. He had been told that often: 'an ideal for young men to follow. A rare and endangered flower in this decadent age,' Sheikh Hafiz at the mosque had proclaimed. Look at the way he spent his day: with the first call of the muezzin he was out of his bed performing his ablutions (until recently in cold water) for dawn prayers. Even though they were not –

strictly speaking – a requirement: just a gift from himself to God. Then he would sit down to his desk and prepare the lectures for the day ahead until the time came for the morning prayers. Again he would lay out his prayer-rug and prostrate himself, adding two prostrations to the prescribed four for good measure. He would choose his clothes. He had three pairs of grey trousers and six white shirts and six pairs of grey socks and one pair of black leather shoes. In winter he would also wear a grey sweater with a V-neck. And he had a dark blue suit and a red-and-blue-striped tie for special occasions, like yesterday's funeral. His eyes rested on the small mirrored wardrobe where his clothes were kept. She kept them so neat; always laundered, smelling fresh, never a button missing and the shoes always polished – and he never saw her do it. All he knew was that whenever he looked, there they all were laid tidily in his cupboard. 'Someday,' he heard his mother's voice saying, 'she'll make some good man a wife worth her weight in gold.' A spasm shot through his stomach and he looked down quickly at his beads. 'O Powerful God, I ask for nothing but patience and am grateful to Thee even for the ills that befall me.'

He concentrated again on the details of his life. After dressing, he would come out of his room to find his breakfast laid on the table in the hall. Naming God, he would sit down and eat. Stewed beans in oil and lemon, warm brown bread and honey, washed down with dark sweet tea. Faten would already be out at school. She had a long journey and a school bus to catch. The door of her room would be open. After eating, he would wash his hands and carefully rinse out his mouth. Then he would collect his books and go to his mother's room. She would be sitting quietly in her bed. When his father was alive he used to breakfast with him, then he would kiss his hand and set off for the university. Now, he would go find his mother and bid her goodbye.

'Stay in peace, Mother.'

'Go in safety, my son.'

And he would go. He would walk carefully down the worn, winding stairs, keeping his eyes lowered in case any of the neighbours' women were about. Then out into the glare and dust of the street. He would walk briskly to the top of the road and wait at the bus-stop. When the bus came the crowd surged forward, each person trying to find a foothold on the steps that were already bent under the weight of bodies. He was young and strong and almost always got on and even managed to inch his way into the interior.

In the bus it was stiflingly, unbearably hot. Your neighbour's hair tickled your nostril, his foot was on your foot and, sometimes, overpoweringly close, was the scent of the female: a woman could be wedged tightly against him, a breast squashed against his arm, or a posterior pressing into his groin. He would keep his eyes lowered and his body as detached as possible. But it was difficult. And when they got to the university he would fight his way out of the bus, strung up with tension, muttering over and over again: 'God preserve us. God preserve us. I take my refuge in Thee.' At least no one had ever quarrelled with him. Often on a bus a woman would turn and, in a voice shrill with anger, shout at the man behind her to 'collect yourself and move your hand away,' or 'shift a little will you, we're your sisters after all.' And the man would murmur: 'What can we do? It's this damned overcrowding,' while the people around looked on and waited for a fight to develop so they could all join in. They were hell those buses. God's Hell. And the things that happened on them – God protect a woman if she were nervous or shy. She'd be felt up by a hundred hands at once. It was good that there was a school bus for Faten. He had forbidden her to ride the ordinary buses and when she had asked why he had simply said, 'Because I know what goes on in them and it's not for my sister.' She accepted everything he did and everything he said – without question. What will I do when she goes to university? he wondered. There will be no school bus then.

He glanced at the glass panel above the bathroom door. It was still lit and the water-heater hummed on. She must be washing her hair. If he dragged up a . . . his heart leapt to his throat. 'I ask Thy forgiveness and pray for Thy support against the whisperings of the Crafty One.'

He tried hard to concentrate on the ninety-nine names of God: 'the Hearer, the Seer, the Judge, the Just, the Benign . . .' But he had been sitting here, like this, with his white cap and *jalabiyyah*, telling his prayer-beads after the sunset prayers on that evening two months ago. It was the day the water-heater was installed. His father had ordered it and two months after his death it arrived. He had had his bath, and Faten, delighted with the new gadget, was having hers. His mother called him to close the door. She sat in bed, as had become her habit, with a shawl around her shoulders.

'I've been at your aunt's house today,' she began.

'Yes? How is she?' he asked dutifully.

'She's well – thanks be to God. All of them are well.' His mother paused. 'She spoke to me about something.'

'Well, Mother, may it be good?'

'You know your cousin, Isam? He's a graduated dentist now and he's starting to think of opening his own clinic. God willing, he's going to be rich and successful and, as my sister says, who deserves to share his success more than his own cousin, Faten?'

'Faten?'

'What do you think?'

He was surprised. 'She is a child.'

'She's sixteen and in the second secondary. We could have a quiet engagement and then they can wait till she finishes school next year. There would be no disrespect to your father. By then Isam will have started the clinic and they can get married.'

'That's nonsense. Faten . . . Faten's an intelligent girl. My father used always to say that she must go to university. She must complete her education.'

'What is all this education, my son? A girl is destined for marriage and children.'

71

'Education is good, Mother. The Prophet (the blessings and peace of God be upon him) commanded us to seek education even as far as China. You know that. Have you spoken to her about any of this?'

'Faten? Of course not. I thought I'd speak to you first.'

'Well, don't open the subject with her. She's still a child. Let her think of her studies. Marriage? It's not possible.'

'Whatever you say, my son,' his mother said. 'If you want the truth, I don't think she even likes him very much. They always used to quarrel when they were children.'

Sitting on the sofa, the new water-heater singing in the flat, he had gone over the conversation. He was sure he was right. His sister was far too young to be thinking of marriage. Of course it was true that marriage was protection for a woman. Particularly now her father was dead. But Faten was a good girl and not likely to go wrong. And *he* was there to look after her. He looked up as he heard the bathroom door open. The light was behind her. She stood for an instant framed in the doorway. Her face was in the shadow and all he could see was the light, shining through her thin cotton night-dress, silhouetting a curved shimmering figure, while her clean, wet hair clung to her neck. She only stood there an instant but he felt the steam new-released from the bathroom surround him and a great heat rise in his body. At that same moment a loud commotion rose in the street and he turned to look. Faten circled the dining-table and came quickly into his room to lean over the railing of the balcony and see what was happening. A crowd was running through the street and everyone was shouting, 'Thief! Thief!' Even those who were not running stood in the doorways of their shops or on the side-walk adding their contribution to the outcry. Her skin was scrubbed and glowing. She smelt of soap. Her hair was sending droplets of water down the neckline of her night-dress and her feet were bare.

'Did you see the thief?' she asked turning to him, facing him with clear, wide brown eyes flecked with gold; eyes that he had never seen before. Her mouth was slightly parted as she waited for the answer.

'Did you see the thief?' she repeated. And he looked away and down into the street.

'No, no. I see nothing,' he said, and his heart pounded. Everything pounded. The world pounded.

'What will they do to him if they catch him?' There was concern in her voice.

He looked grim. 'Give him a beating first, then take him to the police station.'

'I don't think they should beat him,' she said; 'it's enough to take him to the police station.'

'He's a thief and he should be punished. There are laws and people should not transgress them. Stealing is against the law of both God and Man.' He could hear his voice growing sharp.

'But supposing he's poor and in need?' Her damp hair curled around her neck and as she leaned forward he could see the drops of water follow the curve into the shadow between her breasts.

'They should find out *what* he stole,' she said. 'Maybe he took some food because he was hungry.'

He wanted to put out a hand and catch a droplet on the tip of his finger. He wanted to bend down and catch one on the tip of his tongue. Gently. He would not touch her. Only the water. He swallowed. His hand, gripping, moved on the railing. His elbow shifted slightly. It touched her arm as she leant beside him and he drew away.

'It makes no difference,' he said. 'He has broken the law and he should be punished.'

She was silent. He had used a tone of authority. He was her older brother and he was in his final year at the Faculty of Law. In time he would be a great barrister or a public prosecutor.

The noise had died down as the chase went further and further away from the neighbourhood. People still stood expectantly in the street, reluctant to end the episode and go home. Faten sighed and drew herself up. 'I hope they don't catch him,' she whispered and turned and went inside. He stood rigidly against the railing for a long time. He who should guard has stolen. An old, old story. He could see so clearly. Every strand of the wet hair, every shining tooth in the half-open mouth, every drop of water – gliding, first hesitantly, then faster on its path down the illuminated skin – stood out radiant in his mind.

Salah fidgeted on the sofa, uncrossing his legs and

drawing them to one side under him. He had to stop. If he could not concentrate on his prayer-beads, let him concentrate on his good, homely, everyday life. On the things he was supposed to do. His days at the university. He was a good student. Law was a subject that appealed to him. It was orderly and precise and had an answer to everything. It showed Man working out the moral good, the will of God, and following it. He had reached the fourth year and now even had hopes of being appointed to the faculty. He worked hard and spent his time between lecture-halls and the library. He never sat in the cafeteria or loitered in the corridors as the other students did. He never chatted up girls. If one of them spoke to him, he answered in a civil manner. But he did not really know them and he did not really want to. They seemed sullied to him, those outdoor girls. Always a bit dishevelled, windblown, bare feet in sandals covered with dust, voices too loud, manner too argumentative, too familiar. And he had never been tempted to transgress God's law and stare at their persons or covet them. Since he had become a man the only women he had raised his eyes to were those he could look at without sin, with impunity, because they were forbidden to him: his aunts, his mother and his sister. Faten. So different from all other girls; her face innocent and trusting, her voice soft and low and shy. Always sparkling clean and smelling of sweet soap as she went about her duties in the house or bent over her desk to do her homework. No flirting, no arguments, just acceptance and respect and love. And what had he done? He had broken God's explicit commandment: 'Your mothers have been forbidden to you, as have your sisters and your aunts and . . .' If Sheikh Hafiz could see inside his heart as he prayed at the head of his friends on Friday he would hound him out of the mosque, and he would be right. He carried filth and contamination in his heart and God would not look with favour on anything he did until he got rid of them.

He thought of himself lurking in the hall, waiting for Faten to pass so he could 'accidentally' brush against her. 'You are our man now. We have no one but you.' His mother's words echoed through his mind. He who should guard has stolen. His fingers touching hers as she hands him the glass of tea. He had become like the furtive men on the buses. How was it that his mother sitting in her big brass bed, her chastely plaited hair hanging over one shoulder, how was it that she did not feel the tremor passing through the room? How could she not feel the heat of the fire burning in his head? And Faten. Did she too feel nothing? Or did she feel it and hide it? Women. They say you never know with women, for they are deficient in brains and morality. Perhaps she feels the same and conceals it. But she seems so innocent. So frank. Her face an open book. Surely she has no secrets, no dark thoughts, no feelings that could not be confessed to. And yet can you really know? Can you ever really know?

The previous night, after the funeral, the friends who had attended persuaded him to go out with them. 'Let's go out and have a good time,' they said. 'Let's forget about death and such morbid things.' They headed downtown and walked among the crowds in Soliman Pacha Street, arms linked, eyeing the women. They found a café in the street and sat down. They ordered tea and chatted in loud voices. About college, about their teachers, but mostly about the girls. As they talked they kept up a running commentary on the women passing in the street. One was thin like a broomstick but had lustful eyes. Another had fair skin, 'like whipped cream' they called after her. A third had a behind like elastic, with a life of its own. At each comment he had found himself thinking of Faten, comparing her with the women passing by, forced to focus on her details. She was not as white as that woman – no – her skin had the glow of ripened wheat, when she walked he never saw her body move with such articulation, she wore loose skirts – but under them – then he would sharply pull his mind away, his fingers working feverishly on the prayer-beads in the pocket of his suit.

Finally, Mus'ad, the one whom he liked least in the group, made a suggestion. 'Let's go to Sawsan's,' he said; 'there is a lovely new girl there. An apple. She's young and looks so innocent, but God, the tricks she knows . . . Whooo!'

'I ask Thy forgiveness, Highest Lord,' he had muttered, clinging to his beads.

'Come on Salah,' cried Mus'ad. 'Stop muttering to yourself and let's go.'

'You are thinking of committing fornication. Of flouting the laws of God.'

'Come on, man. It's just one night. Taste it and see. After all, marriage is the half of religion isn't it, and how can you get married without a bit of training?' He laughed.

'Leave him alone, Mus'ad,' intervened another friend, 'Salah is not like us. He's a man of God.'

'What? Does the flesh have no hold at all over him then? You know what they say don't you? They say these "men of God" are real whore-masters at heart. They could teach you and me things we never even dreamed of . . .'

'I'm going,' Salah had declared. His head was throbbing furiously. No one had dared suggest such a thing to him before. Now they sensed his impurity. It was showing through. God was sending him a warning. He was saying, 'I can see you. And others will too.' He shouldered his way quickly down the crowded street, holding onto the prayer-beads in his pocket. 'God preserve me from the temptation of the Evil One. I beg of Thee to save me – save me from the temptation of that which Thou hast created . . .'

He had reached home without having walked off his turmoil. He had climbed the stairs slowly, looking down at the ground. The muscles of his legs and thighs ached and he breathed heavily. What is the use? What is the use of lowering your eyes and not looking at the neighbours' women if you raised your eyes to your own sister? But it is permitted. It is permitted to raise your eyes to your own sister. And is it permitted to covet her? To lust after her? To try and touch her with your corrupt body and pollute her innocence? How do I know she is innocent? Things are not what they seem. My face is still sharp and clean-boned; my eyes direct and honest. Nobody knows the filth in my heart. How do I know anything? He let himself quietly into the flat. It was past eleven and both his mother and his sister were asleep. Only the night-lamp burned dimly in the hall. He walked straight to his room and started undressing. He had not yet performed the evening prayers. He started to recross the hall to the bathroom to perform his ablutions. In truth he had committed nothing that rendered him unfit for prayer, but he felt he had to cleanse himself after the loose talk at the café. He walked round the dining-table and stopped before his sister's door. It was ajar. She never closed it when she went to bed. She had no secrets. He touched it gently. In silent collusion with him, it inched open. He stepped inside. The blinds were wide open and the room was lit by the neon of the street. In the far corner stood her bed and she slept on it, curled up under a sheet. She was bundled up in the white cotton, completely covered, only her head showing, her hair spread out, her eyes lightly closed. He bent over her. Would she wake up? He could smell the scent of soap and could hear her breath, gentle against the pillow. He put out his hand to touch her and she moved, turning to lie flat on her back, defenceless, open to him. He stepped back. He stood for a moment gazing at the outline of her body under the sheet, then he turned and left the room. He dragged himself round the dining-table and back to his room. Ablutions forgotten, he stumbled onto his bed and fell into an exhausted sleep.

As he awoke to the voice of the muezzin calling for dawn prayers, he had a feeling that something terrible had happened. He had a memory of lifting a sheet, touching a breast. He had a memory of Faten holding him under the sheet, caressing him where he most longed to be caressed. Yet when he had whispered her name she had laughed at him and said, 'My name is Sawsan. Don't you know me?' It was only a dream, he reassured himself, only a dream. But then another realisation hit him. He had gone to bed without performing the evening prayers. For the first time since he had become a man, he had missed a prayer. And now it was gone for ever. You could not carry over prayers from one day to the next. He covered his face with his hands. He was impure, unclean, and his body had a lethargy he had never known before. 'O God,' he prayed, 'help me. I have reached the depths. For the sake of Thy Prophet, help me.'

He was not sure how he had passed the day. He had gone out. He had gone to classes. But he was absent. He did not know what was going on around him. He paid no attention to the lectures and he took no notes. And he had missed all his prayers. It seemed useless. No, it seemed blasphemous to pray while he was so contaminated. He had to find salvation. Then he could pray again.

He sat on the sofa holding the beads, suddenly wary of pronouncing the names of God. His consciousness revolved around one fact: they were alone in the flat. His mother would not be back for another hour yet. The water-heater was quiet. Faten must be drying herself now. Rubbing her body all over. Bending to reach an ankle or raising her leg to the edge of – if he went on like this he would be lost. He would be lost to both this world and the next; his studies and his future would be lost. His soul would be lost.

The bathroom door opened, spilling light and steam into the hallway. Then Faten put out her hand, switched off the light and turned to her room. Surely she was wearing nothing underneath that night-dress. And why did she always come out of the bathroom barefoot? Was it a test? A test sent by God to try him? She came back out of her room with her hair wrapped in a towel. She crossed the hall and came into his room. 'I'm going to make myself some tea. Would you like some?'

'No.'

She stood for a moment, surprised at the shortness of his answer, then she quietly left the room. He could hear her moving in the kitchen. Then she crossed the hall carrying a glass of tea in one hand and a sandwich in the other. She went into her room pushing the door to behind her.

'Dear God, take my hand, support me, help me.'

His mother would not be back for another hour.

Tea, some tea? He would go to the kitchen and make some tea. He got up from the sofa, straightened his *jalabiyyah* and pushed his feet into his slippers. He walked into the hall and over to the kitchen, then he turned back and stopped at his sister's door. He stood waiting. He could hear a rustle of paper. Did she wear nothing at all under that night-dress? He pushed open the door and went in. She was sitting at her desk with her back to him. She turned. He walked up to her slowly and put out his hand and rested it on her bare neck. She smiled up at him. His legs trembled. Beyond her face he could see the desk. On it was a magazine with photographs telling a story. One shot showed a man holding a woman's arm as she strained to get away from him.

'What's this?'

She turned to the magazine. 'This? Oh it's French. Mlle Amal said the best way to learn conversation is to read these magazines and she lent me one for today.'

His hand tightened on her neck. In the picture the woman's breasts were very clearly outlined. 'And what do you think of it?'

'I like it. It's amusing. It makes learning more interesting.' She laughed up at him. 'It's better than doing boring grammar exercises.'

He suddenly pulled her around. 'Do you realise that these are obscene publications? That they are blasphemous?' His voice grew high. 'And you dare sit there and tell me you enjoy them?' His hands are gripping her upper arm now, hurting her. The backs of his fingers touch the side of her breast. His hand tingles and hums. 'Is this what we send you to school for? To learn rudeness and obscenities? I'll go to that school tomorrow and see what that teacher of yours thinks she's up to.'

'But, Salah, you don't understand –'

The blow to her right cheek swings her head around. The towel slides off her head and her wet hair comes tumbling down around her neck.

'Shut up. I'll tell you when to speak. You've been having your own way for too long now. You haven't been watched closely enough to see what you're turning into. Well that's all over now, do you hear that?' His hand is in her hair. 'I'm wise to you and to your little ways now and I'll put a stop to them. Do you hear me? You may be fooling everyone but you're not fooling me.' Dry eyes wide open, Faten stares at him. He shakes her. 'Why are you staring at me?' he shouts. 'Have you never seen me before? Or is it because you know I've found out about you? You pretend to be so innocent. We'll soon see how innocent you are –' The water from her hair trickles down his hand. He releases her arm and his hand moves across her breast to the neck of her night-dress. She sits still. A key turns in the lock and their mother, shrouded from head to toe in black, walks in.

'Whatever's the matter, Salah? I could hear your voice all the way down the stairs.'

He lets go of his sister and turns to his mother. He passes a hand over his eyes. Faten, released, rushes over to the bed and lies down. She curls up and faces the wall, drawing the sheet over her.

'Come into your room a minute, Mother. I want to talk to you.' His voice shakes. He follows his mother into her room and closes the door.

'Remember you spoke to me about Isam? Does he still want her?'

'I suppose so . . .'

'Let's marry her to him.'

'But her education? Did you not say . . .'

'All this education will do her no good. I caught her reading an obscene publication tonight. In French. And if she goes to university she'll be ruined like all the girls there. I don't want to see my sister with red nails. With a loud voice and a brassy stare.'

'Well . . . shall we wait till she finishes school next year?'

'If she's not going to university why does she need to finish school? She is not going to go out to work is she? No. The sooner the better.' His voice steadies. 'If she really wants to she can always study at home – later.'

'You don't think she's too young? You said –'

'She's over sixteen. That's the age the law specifies and there must be a good reason for it. No. Let it be done quickly. Doesn't he want her?'

'Of course he wants her.'

'Well then. Marriage is protection. Let's do it quickly and she can move in with her aunt until he finds a flat. I've been thinking about this a lot and I am sure I'm right.'

'Whatever you say, my son. You're the man in this house.'

'You'll speak to my aunt tomorrow?'
'Of course. She will be delighted. And so will Isam.'
'May God bring this to a happy conclusion, Mother.'
'Amen, O God of the two worlds, *inshallah!*'
He walked from his mother's room into the bathroom and turned on the cold tap.

MANDY

Wednesday, 28 December, 1978

Dear Mummy,

I am writing to you from New York – although by the time you get this I'll be back in London. We're visiting (or 'visiting with' as they all say) some friends of Gerald's. He had his heart set on coming here for the New Year, so here we are. This is our third day here and I haven't really seen anything of the city yet – but I will soon –

I saw Saif in London just before I left and he seems OK. I found I envied him his pretty flat dreadfully. This trip has put off my accommodation problem for a bit – but I think Gerald and I are beyond working things out (did you know all along?) and I'm going to try and find a place of my own as soon as I get back to London –

although there *is* something quite bracing about having all my possessions in the car and being 'of no fixed address'.

Gerald doesn't think so at all, of course. He's ravenous for the three-bedroomed house – preferably in the Boltons – and the garageful of Porsche. Maybe he'll get them some day; I wish him luck but I'm truly fed up with him being angry with me for 'having once had them' –

Anyway. Saif has got himself a lean-looking one too. Female, of course. And American. Yes. I'm afraid the days of Lady Caroline of the tiger-shooting, coolie-whipping father are over and the chances of her riding for the Gezira Club as plain Mrs Madi have quite disappeared. He brought this new one too up North in my last fortnight – when I was printing out the thesis. He was taking her on the Windermere round. To a little hotel run by two gay chaps where we once had dinner. He was taking her there for a couple of days and phoned me and said could he come up and borrow the Lancia? And I said I'd rather he took it because I was going to be finishing soon and how was I going to drive two cars away from that place? So they came up on the train and I met them. I paid two pence and went down to platform three as I had done so many times before and the train came in and he stepped out as he had done so many times before – and, as usual, he was a bit shorter than I remembered and, as usual, I wasn't quite sure what I was doing there, and then she stepped out after him and solved my problems. She was dressed up like a Lichfield ad. A Country Casual outfit that he'd wanted me to buy back in 1975: a just-below-the-knee camel skirt, a russet cashmere jumper and a *cape* – would you believe – with a Burberry check scarf, brown Charles Jourdan boots and an Etienne Aigner handbag to match. She even had fawn gloves. She looked terribly lost inside all that. It didn't suit her at all. Anyone could see he had only just bought it for her. Her name is Mandy. She's the small-boned wiry NY type. Arty-looking with frizzed-out brown hair, an amazingly clear, lit-up kind of skin and a very slight cast in her left eye which is actually quite appealing.

Anyway, seeing her in those clothes was weird. They're just the kind of thing he's always thought elegant women should wear and I'm sure she would never, ever have chosen them for herself. Do you remember that scene I told you about in Harvey Nichols where he stopped in front of a mannequin and said, 'That would look good on you,' and I started to cry and kept asking, 'Why does it always have to be beige?' Well, seeing this free-wheelin', verse-writin' (he says she is a poet and a photographer – both!), dope-smokin' (you mustn't be shocked, Mummy, everybody does it here. And you mustn't worry: I'm not doing it) New Yorker dressed like English County brought that side of it all back to me and I was so relieved to be through and out. But I must admit I felt a pang of jealousy: it was the idea of him 'looking after' her, I guess. Like seeing you or Daddy being really nice to someone other than me! I mean, I wasn't *jealous* jealous:

I didn't want to swap places with her or anything – and I certainly didn't wish her any harm – I felt sorry for her: she looked so out of place, so uneasy and so determined. I suppose it must be rough being dragged off to meet 'the wife' – even an 'estranged' wife – as he once put it. (Neither of us has mentioned a divorce yet.)

Anyway, he was looking great: better than any time since we got engaged. He's stopped trying not to smoke and is back to forty cigarettes a day, except its Freiburg and Tryer now not Rothmans. He's terribly chic and he's in a bearded phase. He looks like a gentleman sea-captain. We all shook hands and smiled and I asked about the journey and we said they'd picked a lovely day for it, then I took them to the best that the town had to offer in the way of cafés – a large room full of senior citizens and irate young mothers – and it all smelled of frying and they, in their Bond Street outfits, looked like posh relatives come to give a poor student a treat.

So, we had tea and I felt terribly like some mother being shown her son's new girl and like a mother I thought, she's not good enough for him, which she isn't. She isn't pretty enough and she doesn't have that unwavering serenity which he needs. She probably is in love with him; it's hard not to be. But also I think she's edgy and restless and won't be happy with him and won't make him happy. I also fear there must be some gold-digging element there because she's so obviously on the make and he looks so prosperous. I don't think his money can possibly last very long, though. A year maximum – and I don't know what he'll do then.

Well, they drove off to the Lakes, a battery of cameras on the back seat and all that. And he phoned to say the hotel was every bit as lovely as we had thought it was when we had dinner there with Mario two and a half years ago. Three days later he came back alone to say goodbye. He said he'd left her in town to do some shopping – but who on earth was going to shop in a little town in the North when they could shop in London in a couple of hours? She just didn't want to go through the meeting-the-wife routine again and I don't blame her –

Windermere, England
11/24/78

She met us at the station and she was so friendly I could have thrown up. Eastern inscrutableness, I guess. Her name is Asya. It actually means 'Asia' in Arabic. *He* says it can also mean 'the Cruel One' and 'she who is full of sorrow'. She insisted on taking us for tea at this dump that reeked of stale frying oil – except, of course, neither of them would know what that was. They must have thought it was 'quaint' and 'picturesque' because it was down a dirty, cobbled lane backing onto the market-place. Everybody else there was either some bearded old woman out for her week's supply of cheap cabbages or a harassed young mom with overloaded baskets and pushchairs. People that couldn't go anywhere better. It was a hell of a depressing scene. (It was like a parable, actually: Youth on its Way – through a Lousy Life – to Old Age. It makes me wonder why we all bother to go on.)

We sat there picking at some greasy pastry and drinking over-boiled tea and making dumb conversation:

She: It's quite a long trip up from London really, is it not?

Me: You must have made it lots of times?

She: At least twenty I should think.

That kind of thing.

Except then they got started on Sadat's Jerusalem trip and couldn't stop – well, finally, she asks for the bill and holding it between two slim, brown fingers, she raises her eyebrows with just the hint of a smile (very charmingly done).

'This is hardly worth fighting over, is it?'

She left what must have been a 50 per cent tip and handed over the car keys on – natch – a solid gold key-ring.

'It's really beautiful up in Windermere. I'm sure you'll have a lovely time.'

She didn't quite say 'children' but she easily could have. And, of course, she was careful not to mention the name of the hotel or let on if she'd been up here with him.

'If you would just drop me off at the house?'

But he wanted to stop by his college first.

He says she's finishing a dissertation: getting a Ph.D – only the way he says it you're not sure if it's a joke or what. (I'm trying to be completely fair here. I'm always 100 per cent honest in my journal – otherwise what's the point of keeping it?) She is good-looking; not a stunner or anything, but OK with a lot of shiny black hair with a loose wave in it. I think she's older than me but I could not guess at her precise age: I never can with Eastern people.

Once we get to the college he wants to go for a walk. All it is is a small-town campus and we keep bumping into people who know him and all he says is 'This is Mandy' and they nod and smile politely and don't say 'Mandy who?' I'm getting pretty fed up by then: this was billed as a trip to the Lake District not down Memory Lane. I don't say anything though, because if I've learnt anything by now I've learnt that he moves at his own sweet pace and does what he wants and screw the rest of the world – and if the world objects or has something different in mind – why then screwing it is just that much more fun. So I trail around after him and smile and say 'Uh-huh?' and 'Hi' and get madder and madder.

Then I get to thinking he wouldn't be taking me round this place if he was planning on splitting soon, would he? And so I'm not mad any more. I can't really afford to be mad at him anyway. For one thing, he's paying for this suite. (I've never stayed in a suite before. It's great. Like now I can't sleep but I don't have to lie next to him in the dark or camp out in the bathroom: I can sit out here in this very beautiful 'olde English' room with the fire gently dying in the grate – this is really a room to write poems in. But I must carry on with this because I haven't been getting much chance lately. Also I feel that this is IMPORTANT and I want to always remember how it felt.)

He's paying for this trip. He pays for everything. Ever since I met him three weeks ago I've never once had to use my own money. Which is just as well since all I've got is my ticket home and five $100 traveller's cheques stashed away – what's left of two years of saving. Except not all that five hundred dollars is really mine. There is:

$14.00   Owed to Clark for one week's rent when I moved out so fast. Unless he managed to let the room right away.

$50.00   Borrowed from Jackie in Paris – to be collected when she comes over.

$20.00   Acid in Amsterdam (alliteration!) – for Don when he comes over.

So that really leaves me with $416.00 that I can honestly call my own. Wow! That wouldn't last two days the way we're going. He must have stashes and stashes of dough the way he throws it around. He thinks what you do when you run out of clean socks is go down to Harrods and buy another two dozen pairs. (The reason he runs out of socks is he changes three times a day. I used to think Arabs weren't very particular about all that – but this guy is paranoid with showers and clean clothes. Also all his socks are black!) All this shopping suits me fine. He's always bought me something too. Like the outfit I was wearing this morning. I was right to wear it because it's called a 'Lady's Travelling Outfit', and that's what I was doing – travelling. I saw her clocking it, right there in the station. I guess it looks kind of new: the creases sharp and the nap all going in one direction and all that. She probably knows the sort of thing he'd buy as well. You're not married to someone for six years without knowing that. Not that you'd think it from the jeans and sweater she was wearing. But then she doesn't need to bother any more. He doesn't mind spending his money on me. He does it like it was the most natural thing in the world. Maybe that's Eastern too: women being chattels and all that. (Does 'chattel' have anything to do with cattle? Maybe because the possessions of nomadic peoples would probably be livestock.) I wonder how much of that I really can put up with? It's quite good fun so far but it's only been three weeks. She must have got fed up with it, though – and she was born to it.

Why the hell do I have to keep on thinking about her? I wonder how much *he* thinks about her? A fair bit I'd guess – although he'd never admit it. Admit it? He'd never discuss it even. He'll maybe answer a straight question – but not always.

But seeing him with her today was really something: he was like some kid showing off. Showing off to his mom. And playing her up. One minute he'd be all intimate half-smiles and the next he'd be needling her. And she all serene and beautiful – taking it all. It's sick if you ask me. Sick. It could have been beautiful: two people – having passed through the Storm that Made their Marriage and then the Storm that Wrecked It – left with a Deep and Intimate Friendship. But in their case it's just sick. I don't know why.

Wow! I got upset just then.

Man, I'd go crazy without this journal. I had a smoke and a small Scotch and here I am again. I put everything in here: accounts, observations, fragments, poems (must remember to copy out two written on – Amsterdam London train), even the days I get my period and the nights I make love.

Talking of making love, I just went and looked at him as he lay sleeping. He looks so peaceful when he sleeps. Not everyone does. Clark grinded his teeth all night. But Saif just turns onto his side and curls up like a baby. I've lain for hours staring at his back: the colour of light caramel candy. Sometimes I'd like to lick it but I don't know what he'd think of that. He's into some kind of Eastern thing he says is called *carezza*: it involves him doing things to me very slowly (nothing weird or far-out; just stroking and things) and me doing nothing at all. It's not a problem since I orgasm at least once each time but I don't always see what's in it for him.

He's very cute though – as well as being rich. Once or twice he's acted strange: all gloomy and smoky and wouldn't speak at all, but mostly he's fun to be with – except I don't always know if he's joking or what. He won't ever talk – I mean really TALK – about anything personal but I guess it takes time to build up communication.

MANDY

What I'd like to do now is take a photo of him sleeping. The flash would wake him though and I haven't got my tripod and his kit is down in the car. I'll take lots of shots of him tomorrow. Maybe I'll take a shot of him taking a shot of me. No, that should be a third person really, to make the point: a third person taking a photo of two people, hiding behind their cameras, shooting each other, with the trees and the fallen leaves all around them and the lake in the background.

Well, I guess we'll have a nice day tomorrow. I don't know if he will want to go on the lake but we'll drive around it and he said there was a neat place in Wordsworth's home town where we could have tea – that means tea and cakes here. I ought to go to bed if I'm going to be in any kind of shape in the morning. But I'm not sleepy. What I'd really like right now is a joint but I'm fresh out. OK. What I'll do is I'll copy out these two poems now, then go to bed.

A Russian dissident sits across from me in the park.
He must be a dissident because
he's Russian, and he's
here
in New York City.
Does he know that Central Park
is
muggers only
after dark?

SANDPIPER

A woman with a toddler walks past
if you can call it
walking:
that motherbaby dance.
Right and left he staggers
leading
distracted
only going forward diagonally
by chance.

Soon I'll pack my camera
my notebook
my ball-point
and come 'home' to
where
she still combs her hair
for you.

You dig, you say, my fishnet tights
my jaunty ass
my cigarette
but now I sit and wonder
do wives wear fishnet tights – in Russia?

I've cheated a bit here because I've worked on the poem
before copying it out. I only had the first two sections
and the ending was different. But I think it's a lot better
like this.

It really is strange how poems work. On an Amsterdam boat-train I remember Central Park and I start a poem. A month later, I add in something from today and – wow! It's there.

I think I have something good here. When we go back to London I'll type it up and start a folder so I can show it to him. This journal stays locked. I don't do poem number two now. I go to bed.

Sunday, 12 March, 1979

Dearest Mummy,

Thank you thank you *thank you* for your letter and for everything in it. Can I be independent and have – at the same time – a guardian angel? You'll be glad to know – *will* you be glad to know? – that everything is moving pretty fast. I've actually started at Citadel Publishing – although we haven't really agreed a salary yet (Vivien tells me I should hold out for more than they're offering) and I've used your money – as you said – to make a down payment on a little flat in Kensington. It's terribly sweet – or will be when it's ready. I'm supposed to move into it next month. Meanwhile – you'll never guess – I'm borrowing Saif's flat while he's away. It feels really odd being in his atmosphere again like this. He's in the States. I don't really know what he's doing there – except he's taken Mandy (I told you about her visit up North) with him. He could be 'meeting her folks', or he could be getting rid of her. I don't know – he gave me a portfolio of her '*oeuvres*' a while back –

*   *   *

Asya pauses and looks up from her typewriter. Maybe that's not fair. After all, Mandy was – presumably – doing her best. And she probably didn't ask Saif to give it to her. Maybe she was horrified at the idea. No. If she'd been horrified it wouldn't have happened. Saif would hardly have pressed her. Asya can just see them: Mandy going on about it – about the possibility of getting it published, Saif finally saying, 'I can give it to Asya if you like; she's in publishing.'

'But what am I supposed to do with this?' Asya had asked.

'I haven't the foggiest,' Saif said.

'I mean, I'm not – well you *know* Citadel isn't that kind of publisher. They do school books –'

'Send her a nice rejection slip,' he said. 'That'd be something.'

Asya picks up Mandy's portfolio – again. Had he particularly wanted her to see this? Was there a message in there somewhere?

A set of photographs of buildings with mirrored windows, and on the facing page:

We see what
we want
to see.
You
see
your own
reflection.

A set of photographs of trees – autumnal – and a blurred figure, Saif surely, vanishing into the distance, and on the facing page:

Next year
once again they
will flower.
You
will not
return.

Asya sits back in her chair. Is this meant for her? But it was Mandy who wrote it, not Saif. Does this mean that whatever had been written she would still have turned it into a personal message? She gazes out of the dark window. Last month she had stood out there; under that tree which now she can only make out as a dark shadow on the other side of the road – and she had watched him. She had watched him and known that she could not go back, sit companionably in the twin armchair and reach for a magazine. She leans sideways trying to see the sky; to see if there are any stars. Imagine the world out there – full of signals. You pick one up – and it seems to speak to you. To you alone. Is this how horoscopes work? If she were to ask him – Asya has to smile; it's exactly the type of question he hates. And yet he sends her this – this portfolio.

She turns back to the table. Gerald would like it. Gerald would *love* it. It's just his kind of thing. Multi-media too. She flicks through the pages and comes again to the longest of the poems and stops, as before, at the last verse. 'So,' she says out loud, 'she can say "ass". Well big deal. Anyone can say "ass". I can say it. "Ass." "Jaunty ass." Big deal.' She turns back to her typewriter.

– and they're vaguely OK I suppose. Not my kind of thing. Anyway, Mummy darling, you're going to have to come over next summer –

SATAN

'I don't understand anything. Are you both joking or what? Do you think I've gone senile that I can't get a straight answer from either of you? So my son is crazy; he's got an armoured head. I know that, but I know also that he treasures you like the light of his eyes and he could never do without you. Yes, I know there's a woman: some low creature has pulled him for two or three weeks; absence does terrible things, child, and it was you who chose to put countries between you. I'm not making excuses for him. Don't ever think that. I am *furious* with him. I've *told* him and I've *sworn*: after this time I'll not enter a home of his until things are all right between you. I'll not enter any home of his unless you are its mistress –'

'Tante,' Asya says, when she can edge a word in, 'Tante. It's not like that. What's happened between Saif and me is nothing at all to do with Clara.'

'Clara! And you can put her name on your tongue?
Your nerves, my dear, your nerves!' Adila Hanim's
voice pitches a couple of notes higher. 'I tell you I didn't
even believe him when he told me you knew.' She
reaches for a casserole dish on a high shelf and before
her daughter-in-law can move to help her she has
banged it down on the cooker. 'She actually has the
boldness to come here with him – what does she think?
She imagines I'm going to welcome her? That we're all
going to sit down together and talk about this and that?
I wouldn't even shake her hand –'

Asya stands in the doorway of the kitchen, her back
leaning against her arms which she has folded behind
her. 'Well, you must have annoyed him then,' she says
gently.

'Let him be annoyed. It's time someone annoyed
him. Staying with her in a hotel – openly – when he
knows I'm coming –'

Beyond her mother-in-law's solid figure, a tall narrow window stands ajar. Visible beyond it is daylight,
and a brick wall. But Asya knows that it opens onto the
narrow passage between the two Victorian houses. To
the right is the fence which encloses the gardens, to the
left is the street.

'But, Tante, she was living with him here. He went
to a hotel because he left the flat for you. It was natural
that he should take her with him.'

'Asya! Are you trying to give me a stroke?' Adila
Hanim pauses with her hands on the rim of the pot into
which she has just thrown a knob of butter. She stares

reproachfully at her daughter-in-law. Why is Asya defending him? Like this, she, Adila, finds herself attacking Saif more and more; as though the matter gnawed at his mother's heart more than at his wife's. She looks at Asya who tries to manage a small smile. She has changed. In the five years since they last met, she has changed. When Asya first came in, and they hugged each other, then drew away with moist eyes, she had thought her daughter-in-law was still the same. But now she sees the changes. The black hair keeping more of its wave than it had ever been allowed in Cairo, the skin paler, the face newly defined, as though it had been sculpted out of its old childish roundness. But above all, the detachment, the holding back, to be seen in the eyes and in every stance of that slim body. Oh, child, child, whatever has happened to you? Adila Hanim turns away.

'He could have stayed with me,' she says.

'With you, Tante, yes. But with you and Hussein and Mira and her mother? There's only one bedroom here. I can't think how you're managing.'

'Look, my dear,' Adila Hanim sighs as she starts chopping an onion into a bowl, 'I didn't want them to come. I've been hearing for a while that there are problems between you two so I thought I'd come over to try and mend things. Then Hussein, God preserve him, says, "Mama, I won't let you go alone; I'm coming with you." The next thing I know his wife is coming too – because she might as well shop for the baby – and then Souma Hanim decides to come and help her daughter with the shopping – so here we are. And the place is tight; I mean the rooms are nice and big but there's only two of them so we're all in each other's throats all the time. I know it's only for a few days but I'm not used to this, child, I'm not used to this.' She shakes her head sadly and bangs her knife against the edge of the bowl to shake off the last of the diced onion.

Asya presses back against the wall. She has not seen Tante Adila for five years and although the brown hair still bravely holds its colour, the face is more troubled and lined than she remembers. She must feel her daughter-in-law's new-found hardness. She must be hurt by it. But Asya isn't hard, not really. She longs to go over and put her arms around those solid shoulders and – and then what? Then they'd sit down and cry together. And in the end Asya still would not be able to give her mother-in-law the thing she wants most; the thing she's come all the way to London for. She watches as Adila Hanim turns on the tap.

On a corner of the ornately tiled floor, a small black kitten is chasing his tail. He is obviously having a lot of fun. Autotelic fun, thinks Asya; all he needs is his own tail – which is fortunate since his own tail is all he's got. She's seen him before: he'd been around when she came here eleven days ago to give Saif some of the mail that kept arriving for him at her address. For a few minutes of her visit the kitten had been a small black ball of fur on her husband's immaculate white shoulder. Clara, he told her, his latest friend, had found this kitten and adopted him. He'd also said

that Clara would have loved to meet her but had gone
out. She was Scots, he said, and spoke with 'och' and
'wee'. Her photo on the desk showed a dreamy, creamy,
oval face and a tumbling mass of auburn hair.

'What was I saying? Yes, I did not speak to her at all,'
Adila Hanim repeats. 'I had to offer her tea of course
because, after all, this counts as my home while I'm
here and she was in it. But apart from that I pretended
not to even see her.'

'It's not her fault, Tante,' Asya begins weakly –

'Why are you defending her?' Adila Hanim shakes
the water from her hands, wipes them on the front of
her apron and puts them on her waist as she turns
around to face her daughter-in-law. Asya looks down at
her shoes, a plain, deep green, away from the sadness
and puzzlement on the careworn face.

'Explain to me,' Adila Hanim says, 'I tell you I just
don't understand any more.'

'Well, what I mean is,' Asya shifts against the wall,
'she isn't the first. There were others before her and
there are going to be others after her. She's just not
terribly important – and anyhow, we had already left
each other.'

'Left each other! Spit from your mouth, child. It's
just a little quarrel and it will pass. He'll get rid of the
red-headed tart.'

'She's not a tart.' Asya realises how odd she must
sound. Either mad or phoney. 'What I mean is,' she
goes on, 'it's sort of normal here. I mean, she met him
and he was a single man – separated. I think she's in

love with him. She probably thinks he's going to marry her.'

'Marry her! He'll have to kill me first. Marry a daughter of a – a woman who'd take a respectable man off his wife? Living abroad has addled your brains, child. That's what's happened.'

Adila Hanim peels potatoes in silence. The kitten flicks its tail, pounces at it, and loses it. Asya watches. She had offered to help but had been waved away. Should she insist? Should she be here at all? She knows the conversation isn't going the way Tante Adila wants it to but then it never could have. Can she stand here and say she'd been unhappy for years? Say she's 'known' another man – but has left him? Say she loves Saif but she has to be free?

When he'd phoned her to say that his mother was in London and wanted to see her they had both known that Adila Hanim was here to try and put an end to the separation between them.

'If you don't want to go that's fine. I'll tell her,' Saif offered.

'No, I'll go. I ought to, and I'd like to see Tante.'

'I'm not going,' he said. 'She'll have dinner laid on and it'll be hellish.'

So here she is. She had known she'd have to stall on any intimate conversation. Yet she really loves Tante Adila – and has missed her – misses her even more now that she's here. Maybe she had hoped somehow to make her feel not too bad about the whole thing. Well. This was a far cry from the days shared in the Madi's kitchen at home: the french doors open onto the garden where the three cats snoozed under the pear tree. Dada Nour preparing the vegetables, her daughter at the sink washing chopping-boards, mixing bowls, graters as they were finished with. Tante and she at the table. Tante cooking; showing her how to rub the boiled pasta with raw egg before covering it with the sauce bolognese; how to recognise the exact moment when the pepper sizzling in the butter was ready for the rice. Tante hadn't thought *she* was a tart for visiting her son; for spending days in their home without her own parents knowing; for vanishing into his room for the afternoon.

'If you love my son,' she once said to her, 'you are loved by me.' What would she say now if she knew the truth? Should she tell her the truth? She looks at her mother-in-law's grieving, betrayed face. What is the truth but every detail of the last nine years? How can it be told? And would it really make this easier? And anyway, shouldn't it be up to him? This is his family. Let them believe what he chooses for them to believe. Maybe he prefers the cad's role to that of the injured husband. She looks down at the kitten, busy now with a stray pistachio nut. Poor Clara. Bad luck to be the one around when this family disciplinary expedition descended.

A little while ago it would have been Mandy. And before that, Lady Caroline. But it was just this gentle, tragic-faced girl's luck. Clara's medieval features made Asya think of the Lady of Shalott. True, she had only seen her photo – but she felt as if she knew her. She knows, for instance, that Clara is dreaming of a home in the shadow of the Pyramids, of 'bonny wee bairns' with brown skins and green eyes. She also knows for a certainty that within two months she'll be back in St Andrews – possibly with a black cat.

Adila Hanim turns and catches Asya staring at the kitten. 'Imagine. She's got a special comb for that cat. A special comb!' She snorts, then shakes her head and goes back to chopping the potatoes into the almost-ready chicken casserole.

When Asya arrived, Adila Hanim had been sharing the kitchen with her second son's mother-in-law, Souma Hamim. Each woman was determined that she would be the one to do all the cooking, the cleaning and the washing-up. Adila Hanim – whose mother had died when she was five leaving her a father and an older brother to look after – because she had never been and never could be in a house run by another woman. Souma Hanim because she was well-bred to an extreme and would never allow it to be said of her that she had sat around and let her daughter's mother-in-law slave over the sink and the stove. So the two women, trying to work in this cupboard which called itself a kitchen and which was a fraction of the size of the rooms they were accustomed to, had been bumping into each other, reaching across each other, easing past each other, urging each other to go for a walk with your son/daughter on this beautiful June day; to go and rest in the living-room and I'll make some tea because there's only one apron, one carving-knife, one grater and anyway, everything's almost ready.

Asya's arrival broke the deadlock. It was obvious her mother-in-law would wish for a word with her in private, and since Hussein was in the living-room and Mira was in the bedroom, it was now possible for Souma Hanim to retire with grace and tact and go check on her pregnant daughter.

'Anyway,' Adila Hanim says, putting the lid firmly on the simmering casserole and grinding pepper into the butter heating for the rice, 'anyway – I'm going to give him a few words when he gets here today. And Hussein intends to speak to him too. It's true he's only his younger brother but circumstances force our hand.'

'He might not be coming, Tante, you know –'

'He's coming, dear. I've told him.'

Mira appears in the kitchen doorway. Mira is seven months married and five months pregnant and this, she feels, gives her an advantage over her senior sister-in-law who has been married for five years and has only a miscarriage to her name. Her importance had become evident to her not so much when she first learned she was pregnant, or when her tummy began to swell and her breasts to grow tender, but when she felt the baby kick inside her. She knew then that she was in possession of an immense and secret power. When she lay in bed that night, and the baby celebrated the freedom afforded to it by this position, she reached for her husband's hand and placed it – to his delight

and wonder – on her gently thumping belly. At that
moment, as far as she was concerned, he relinquished
his priority position in the household: Baby came first,
she, the Bearer, came second and her husband last. No
wonder then, that she who used to jump up so eagerly,
could now sit back and let her mother-in-law remove
her empty glass of tea, take it to the kitchen and wash
it. No wonder that she could sit placidly, her hand on
her stomach, vaguely aware of her husband fixing his
own supper-tray in the kitchen. And no wonder again
that – feeling she had the sacred words, the unanswer-
able argument that would right all wrongs between her
husband's brother and his wife – she should touch her
sister-in-law's hand saying, 'I want to talk to you' and
precede her into the bedroom.

Asya is surprised because she and Mira only met an
hour ago and she cannot imagine that this newcomer
thinks she has anything to contribute to this already
crowded situation. She glances at her mother-in-law,
but Tante Adila is busy with the rice and trying to look
as though it were an everyday happening for her two
daughters-in-law to engage in girlish tête-à-têtes. Asya
follows Mira into the bedroom and pushes the door to.
Both women sit on the edge of the bed. There is
nowhere else to sit.

Mira's eyes follow her own finger as it traces the
ridges on the purple candlewick bedspread. Asya folds
her own hands on her knees and waits. She has not
particularly taken to Hussein's wife. One would think
Hussein could have done better for himself than this

puffy, solemn girl. He is very good-looking – the handsomest maybe of the three Madi brothers – and knows it; he always wears a gold chain around his neck and his moustache trimmed just so, and he'd always been big with the girls at the club and at college. How odd, after all the jokes they'd shared, all the football matches they'd cheered together in the large, cool living-room of his parents' house, after the fire-lit dinners, the camp-beds she'd fixed him in the north of this country, how odd that he should now be sitting out there, in his brother's rented living-room, with a newspaper, like a stranger. He had not spoken except to greet her and had merely shaken her hand politely when he opened the door. She sensed his puzzlement, and also his disapproval. Come to think of it though, they'd never actually had any *real* conversations, and whenever he'd expressed an opinion – which he hadn't often done – it had always been more restrained, more ordinary, than she'd expected. Also, as far as she knew, he had never, ever, brought a girl home. She would not have lacked a welcome, for – although Asya distinctly got the feeling that Mira did not get on well with her mother-in-law – Tante Adila was the most open-hearted and hospitable of women, reserving her small store of animosity exclusively for Tante Durriya, the wife of her worshipped older brother. Maybe Hussein deserves his ponderous, silent, doubtless well-dowried bride, she thinks.

Across the room, by the french windows, unopenable onto the back patio, a dark patch begins to unfold itself on the carpet. It straightens onto four frail legs, steps into a medallion of pale sunshine and stretches itself thoroughly. Then it rolls over onto its back and scrambles again to its feet. Its nose, its ears, its bright yellow eyes and its tail are all quivering with alert curiosity.

'Ah. So that's where you've been.'

Asya bends and scratches her fingernails on the carpet. The kitten is upon them instantly. There they play, the hand and the cat: scratching, advancing, poking, pouncing, retreating, until Mira, stung by this unseemly display of frivolity, straightens up, captures her own wandering hand, rolls it into a fist, coughs slightly and says, 'There are problems between you and Saif?'

Asya glances up. 'Oh no. It's all over. There aren't any problems any more.'

'But I heard – I heard that you're going to leave him.'

The kitten is lying on its back, paws raised, waiting to strike at Asya's hovering hand. Even its belly is jet-black.

'We've already left each other – almost a year ago.'

Asya, tired of bending, scoops Satan onto her knee. He weighs nothing at all.

'But everybody says you love him,' Mira says.

'I do love him,' Asya patiently repeats, 'but not to be married to him.'

Mira's voice is impatient. 'What do you mean?'

Asya looks at the warm black fur on her knee. She strokes its panting side with her thumbs and can feel the

kitten purring. Who is this woman sitting here questioning her? Then she considers that living at home in the
heart of the family, while all this trouble was brewing
abroad, Mira must have heard her – Asya – discussed a
thousand times. She very probably imagines that she
does know her, that they are indeed sisters-in-law. Yet
how can she truly explain anything to her? She sighs.

'I mean that I love him very, very much but that over
the last few years we've grown apart and I don't think
we love each other in the way married people should.
One loves people in different ways –'

She pauses, and Mira cuts in. 'Asya, you're twenty-
nine, aren't you?'

Asya glances at her. 'Yes,' she says.

And now Mira draws out her indisputable, unans-
werable ace. She considers it, then leans forward and
places it gently on the candlewick bedspread. 'Don't
you want to have a baby with him?'

Asya shakes her head slowly, stroking – stroking the
kitten. 'No,' she says.

'No? How do you mean, "no"?'

'No,' says Asya. 'No, I don't.'

After that there is nothing to be said. But to get up
and go would mean that offence had been taken and
besides there is nowhere to go except the living-room
where Hussein sits rustling the *Evening Standard*, or the
tiny kitchen where the mothers-in-law are clanking the
pots. So Mira folds her hands over her belly and lies
back, duty done. Asya is clearly beyond reach and is
probably even 'going' with someone as she hears said,

although Tante Adila always denies it and springs to her first daughter-in-law's defence. But then Tante Adila is a fool where Saif and his wife are concerned.

And why am I so sure? Asya wonders, stroking the kitten, am I really so sure, so completely sure that I don't want his baby? And in her mind, once again, the image forms: there he is, the child she had imagined as she lay on the sofa, all those years ago, willing him to hold on, to stay in the womb. He is two years old, wearing soft, dark, velvet pants and a white T-shirt, his face round and serious and dark-eyed like in the photos of Saif as a baby. His bare, plump feet are planted sturdily on the wooden floor and he is occupied with something, some toy that is obscured from her by the arm of the chair he leans against. He would have been six years old now. She hath miscarried of her saviour, they said of Anne Boleyn. The kitten jumps off her knee and she stands up. No. She walks over to the sealed window and stands looking at the bare but sunlit patio. No. I am not going to start thinking about it all over again. No. It's over. It's really over and I know that it's over. The child is long gone, and the marriage is over, and Saif is all right now. He is over the worst of it. And he's started having girlfriends again. She can think of herself as an interlude in his life; a nine-year interlude. And she is not jealous of them. Not of one. Not Nicola or Jenny, both friends of hers and each taking great trouble that she should not know – as though they couldn't believe she didn't care. Not of Lady Caroline or Mandy or this Scots girl with the creamy skin and the thigh-length hair; Clara, who adopts stray kittens. Poor Clara, who is taking the brunt of Tante Adila's disappointment and displeasure –

The bedroom door is pushed open and Adila Hanim seethes in. The kitten streaks out.

'So he's not coming then or what?'

Adila Hanim is wiping her hands roughly on a kitchen cloth. The lines from the corners of her nostrils, around her mouth and into her chin are etched deep, and her chin has never looked so square and hard as it does now. Asya feels sorry. So sorry.

'But I told you, Tante.'

'Told me what and didn't tell me what, Asya? Last night when I spoke to him he said, "Yes." '

'The word "Yes" saves trouble. Saif always does that.'

'So he's not coming?'

'I – I don't think so.'

'All right. In any case, dinner's ready so you two come and eat.'

Out in the living-room, the table in the wide bay window – the table where he has his 'Bohemian banquets' of a joint of cold meat, ten cheeses, pickles, french bread and red wine – is laid for six. Hussein is already sitting at what seems to have become his usual place: at his mother's left, facing the window. Souma Hanim is ladling out soup from a big white tureen at the centre of the table.

Adila Hanim sets down a large basket of bread rolls, then sits down heavily at the other end of the table from where Souma Hanim is apparently about to sit. Asya moves to sit at her mother-in-law's right.

Mira emerges from the bedroom and takes her place between her husband and her mother. And both the chair and the dish to Asya's right remain empty.

Everyone mutters, '*Bismillah,*' and raises their spoons. After a few mouthfuls, Mira angles her spoon delicately into her dish and sits back. Her mother stops eating. She leans over, staring at her daughter anxiously.

'*Mais qu'est-ce que tu as, chérie?*'

'Nothing, Maman, I've had enough.'

'But you've hardly had any of it!'

'I've had enough.'

Souma Hanim lays her spoon down and reaches out to feel Mira's forehead. 'You don't have a temperature or anything.'

'Did I say I had a temperature?'

Tante Adila is rather noisily finishing the last spoonful of her soup. Hussein has laid his spoon down in his empty dish. Asya feels a soft touch on her ankle. She slips off one shoe and secretly strokes the kitten with her bare foot.

'Well, what's wrong with the soup? Your Tante Adila and I are spending this whole trip in the kitchen for you to take two mouthfuls and leave the rest?'

'Maman, I'm full. I'm full. *Ouf.*'

Tante Souma changes tack. '*Ah, chérie,* take a couple more spoonfuls, darling, for my sake. *C'est un bon potage, ça. Tu dois manger, chérie. Tu dois. Même pour le petit –*'

Tante Adila collects four empty dishes and goes to the kitchen. Hussein, who speaks no French, sits silently staring out of the window.

'Maman, I just don't want any more soup.' Mira clenches her hands and her engagement solitaire glints. Souma Hanim gazes at her daughter.

A crash in the kitchen is followed by a loud and scolding invocation to the Preventer of Disasters. Adila Hanim staggers in using two bunched up kitchen towels to hold a steaming and obviously dangerously heavy casserole. Hussein gets to his feet.

'Shouldn't you have called me to carry that?'

His mother lets the casserole bang down on to the king-size Lady and Unicorn mat in the centre of the table and – without answering – turns around and marches back into the kitchen.

He stands for a moment staring at the empty door-way then, with a slight shrug, sits down and resumes gazing past Asya and out of the window.

'Well then, *tu va manger un peu de ce poulet au casserole?*'

The rice is placed on the table and Adila Hanim sits down with a fresh stack of six plates in front of her. The struggle between the complaints rising within her and the necessity of saving face in front of these two strange women – her second son's wife and his mother-in-law – have compressed her lips into a hard, thin line.

She starts serving. But as she bangs the spoon against the side of the plate to shake off a few grains of rice, she starts to mutter. 'All day long I'm cooking and he doesn't even bother to show up. Well, tell me. Say, "I'm sorry Mama, I won't be able to come." Since when have I forced him? Can anyone force him? Ever? To do anything? Never in his life has it been possible for anyone to make Saif do anything except what he has already inside his own head.'

Asya receives her plate with lowered eyes and murmurs her thanks. She sits, the creator of all this dislocation and misery, and nothing she can say can make anything any better. And leaving won't help either. She can't leave – at least not until she has finished all the food that Tante chooses to give her and sipped at a glass of mint tea. She has to get out soon, though, and she has to avoid any chance of another conversation with Tante. That will definitely happen if she insists (as she should, being the cause of their coming to this servantless country) on washing the dishes. Tante Adila will corner her later in the tiny kitchen and then – and then Asya might break down and tell her everything. So she must just be rude and escape immediately after the tea. Oh, if only Saif were here, he would have stopped his mother at the door and taken the dish from her and scolded her, he'd have talked to Hussein and caught Asya's eye and grinned at the french remonstrances, he'd have held out scraps of food to the kitten, and Tante Adila would have been happy. Oh, if only –

Glancing up from her plate, Asya sees that Satan is in the middle of the table. Keeping his front paws at a safe distance from the hot bowl, he stretches his neck and takes elegantly pointed sniffs at the aroma of stewed chicken.

'*Mange, chérie, mange,*' Souma Hanim whispers solicitously, patting Mira's drooping shoulder. Hussein springs to his feet, his face dark.

'God curse your father, why don't you stay away from us?' he shouts and, grabbing the kitten by the neck, hurls it against the far wall. Asya stands up.

On the floor, in the far corner, the kitten crouches utterly still. Souma Hanim glances up at Hussein, then goes back to concentrating on her daughter, who appears not to have noticed anything. Tante Adila continues to dissect her chicken wing.

'What have you done?' Asya tries to keep her voice low. 'You've broken him. You've broken his back.'

Hussein sits down and puts his elbows squarely on the table. Asya runs around the table towards the kitten. She bends over, not daring to touch it in case it slumps broken in her hand. Slowly and shakily, Satan gets up. He stands on trembling legs, shakes himself, then with a jaunty little leap, he is out of the room. Asya collects her handbag.

'Where are you going, child? Come and finish your food.'

'No. Thank you, Tante Adila, no. What has the kitten done that Hussein should throw him at the wall like that? That's shameful; taking it out on a kitten. What has he done? I'm going, Tante. I'm sorry.'

Asya is close to tears. She drives to Blake's Hotel. She asks for her husband at the desk, and then paces while she waits. He comes down smiling, in a pale, cream cotton shirt and a maroon cravat, with a question in his eyes. What is the question? Is it merely, 'Why are you here?' Or is it, 'Now that you have seen what you are doing to your Tante Adila, are you thinking of coming back?'

'Hi,' she says. 'Look. It's wrong to leave that kitten there. Tante doesn't like him and Hussein is treating him badly.'

'The cat?' He looks blank. 'It's only for a couple of days.'

'In a couple of days he could be dead.'

Saif smiles. 'Hussein is going to murder a kitten?'

'He threw him across the room just now and practically broke his back. I don't think you should leave him there.'

'I can't bring a kitten to the hotel. It's only a couple of days.'

His voice has hardened in that way she knows so well. He is both bored and unyielding. She knows what he is thinking; he's thinking, 'Here's another attack of the dramatics: another of the theatrical fits.' Well, he can think what he pleases; he's well out of it now isn't he? She feels the tears rising to her eyes and knows that she has lost.

'Clara will be miserable if something happens to him,' she says.

Saif reaches in his pocket and takes out a pack of Rothmans.

'You're concerned for Clara?' he asks.

SATAN

The tears spill from her eyes and Asya turns away. She'll take the kitten. She'll go back and pick him up and take him away. It isn't right to leave Satan with these people. It simply isn't right.

I THINK OF YOU

(To Nihad Gad)

I think of you often. I think of you often, and I remember. I remember, for instance, your old nanny coming into your room, the edges of her *tarha* bitten between her teeth to hide half her face. Her eyes, filmed with cataracts, were so dim she must have been seeing you as though through a mist. I remember your husband turning from the phone, and the small gesture of your hand that stilled the impatient words on his lips. The old woman muttered indistinctly as she moved towards you, her arm describing cramped, arthritic circles with the smoking incense-burner. Through the window, the darkness of the Cairo night was so intense, it seemed that if I reached out my hand I would touch black velvet.

SANDPIPER

Now the amber incense pervades this room, and as my eyes track the sweet cloud drifting behind the Baluchi cleaning-woman, I see you once again sitting up in bed, splendid, your head wrapped in a turban of emerald silk. From the sofa I watched you: lit by a discreet lamp, your bed on a raised dais, a huge grey-and-white fur rug thrown over the bedclothes. In my light dress my body was warm with new life, but around your shoulders you drew a dark red woollen cloak and the fingers that held it to your breast were longer, more tapering than I had remembered, although still tipped in defiant scarlet.

Barbarian Queen, I thought then, Medieval Matriarch. Now, beached in this strange country, I wonder what these women amongst whom I find myself would make of you. Five women, each in a bed. They are dressed in greys and browns; garments fashioned so that underneath them they are all identical, solid bulk. Their hair is closely wrapped in dense black cloth, and more black cloth is folded back on top of their heads ready to veil their faces at a second's notice. My white cotton night-dress, smocked, buttoned to my throat, wide-sleeved with a frilled cuff touching the backs of my hands, feels light, revealing, beside the dark layers that they wear. My hair is uncovered and loose. I pull it back and twist it into a half-hearted braid and I feel the movement of my arms making my breasts shift under the cotton. I have nothing with which to secure my hair.

Your head was wrapped in emerald silk. The front still showed a narrow black hairline, but at the back, a thin, smoky tendril had escaped. Your son, fifteen years old, came in and wrinkled his nose at the smell of incense. Your old nanny slowly swung the burner into the corners of the room. Flat on the floor at the foot of your bed your dog lay; he flicked his tail and watched me with sad, uninterested eyes. Your son, before he left the room, climbed the dais to kiss you. Elevated, theatrical, your bed was worthy of Cleopatra; worthy of nights, afternoons, mornings of kingly caresses. And finally, of this.

I push my bare feet out from under the sheet and lower them from the bed. The perfect toe-nails I had once more achieved – twisting, bending, manoeuvring around my now enormous belly – are here ten small, red badges of shame. And as my feet touch the floor, the night-dress slipping to reveal two ankles, swollen, but still ankles, the door of the ward swings open, a warning cough is heard, and a man walks in. Four hands fly up to four heads, four veils drop over four faces, and all sounds cease. Heavily I stand and reach for the curtains as the man, with lowered eyes, walks to the fifth bed and sits by his wife. I am not supposed to move, not supposed to move at all. But I walk slowly around my bed, drawing the green and yellow curtains, plucking at their edges, placing them carefully one over the other to complete my isolation. Awkwardly I climb again into the bed. I lie flat on my back and hold the sheet to my chin. I feel the tears well into my eyes and let them trickle coldly down my temples and into my hair. I do not want to be here.

Your hands were so thin and fine, a network of blue veins showed through the skin. Your eyebrows were carefully shaped: winged high above your deep, black eyes. Your cheek-bones (oh, how I always coveted your cheek-bones) stood out now even more. Your mouth remained the same: wide and strong, the full lower lip tensing as you pulled your cloak more closely around you. Your mother, burdened by years and by her fear for you, stood for a moment in the doorway. Your husband lit another cigarette. You looked at the evening paper and talked animatedly about a review. I sat on the sofa and wondered how you could. But on the other hand, how else could you have been?

The Filipino nurse whisks the curtains apart and stands smiling between them. 'You have to have some air. You will be too hot,' she says, and briskly walks around the bed pulling them wide open. The man by the fifth bed has gone and the women are talking in low voices. The nurse picks up my wrist and stares at her watch. Then she puts my wrist down and shakes out a thermometer. As she puts the thermometer into my mouth, 'You must not cry,' she says on a melodious, rising note. 'Why you are crying? You will be all right.'

Do you cry, my dear? I've never seen you cry. And yet, I think I can hear the great, wrenching sobs – late, late in the night, when all the house is asleep.

One of the women gets out of her bed and walks round to the sink just outside my open curtains and hawks and spits then runs the tap for a moment. She takes the two steps to my bedside and stands looking down at me. 'Do not weep,' she says.

I nod. So what if she spits into the sink? She didn't spit on me.

'Why do you weep?' she says.

I shrug feebly. If I open my mouth I shall howl.

'You do not speak Arabic?' she says.

'Yes, I speak,' I say, but my voice comes out in a shaky whisper. I cannot make her out; with the shapeless smock and the wrapped head she could be anything from eighteen to forty-five.

'Carrying, yes?' she says.

Again I nod.

'What is wrong with you?' she says.

I whisper, 'High blood-pressure.'

'All things are in the hand of God,' she says, and I nod. 'Shall I raise your bed a bit?' she says, 'you cannot be comfortable like this.'

I shake my head; I do not want to be comfortable. But she cranks the bed up anyway so that my shoulders and head are raised up a little. She is being kind. Curious, naturally, but kind too. But I do not want to be comfortable. I do not want anything except not to be here.

I want to be with my daughter. Over the phone she asks, 'Why do we have to be separated like this?' She is five years old and chooses her words with care and I want to be with her, treading water in the middle of a cool swimming-pool, my circling arms breaking up the sun's reflection into patterns that form and re-form while she swims from me to the edge and from the edge to me again. I want to hold her foot as she sleeps; on her back, arms and legs flung out wide, and, in the dim light, watch her eyes move under the delicate, slightly purpled lids and wonder what it is she dreams of.

Standing at the window, I watched your driver and your old doorman kneel together inside your gate for evening prayers. I was sure they prayed also for you. In the street, a young couple loitered arm in arm in the crisp spring air and stared into a shop-front glittering with fancy shoes. Beyond them, I could see the glow of Cinema Roxy and I could almost feel the general hum as the open-air cafés of Heliopolis filled up for the evening. Your husband came up to the bed and looked at your drip. From the sitting-room next door came the hum of conversation punctuated by the periodic click of the telephone followed by a chime as someone hung up and tried yet another number.

The Filipino nurse comes back with a young man in a white coat. The woman standing over me retreats to her bed. The doctor's stethoscope dangles close to my face. He says, 'You must not cry, Madame, it is not good for you.' He speaks with a Syrian accent and kindly, and his eyes are a light hazel but they are too bright. I feel my mouth shape itself into a polite smile and my hand lying by my side makes a slight gesture as though to say it's nothing.

'You must not be afraid,' he says again; 'all things are in the hand of God.'

I nod and close my eyes briefly. I do not trust myself to speak. He stands and looks at me. His mouth smiles and his eyes burn. I wish I could make him less uncomfortable. I move my hand again.

My neighbour in the compound said, 'You can have a crisis at any minute. If you're not in hospital you'll die.' I said, 'If I feel a crisis coming, I'll run to you for help.' 'You won't be able to run.' 'I'll walk then.' 'It's not a joke,' she said; 'you have to go into hospital.' 'How can I go into hospital?' I ask, 'the exams are this week, I have to be with my students.' 'You don't understand,' she says, 'I'm telling you: you'll die.' In the end she brought me in for a check-up, and when they kept me, she took my daughter home with her. She looks after her and they phone me twice a day. When all is said and done, my daughter is the reason I would prefer to stay alive. She, and this other, uncelebrated child inside me, clinging so tenaciously to life.

When your husband and the doctor left the room and we were alone, I climbed the two steps to your bed and picked up the hot-water bottle from where it lay on the fur rug beside you and said, 'Wouldn't it be better under the cover?' I lifted the rug and the quilt and the blanket and the sheet and snuggled the bottle against you and covered you again. I put my hand on your shoulder and said, 'Would you like me to rub your back?' And you sighed, 'Oh, my dear, I wish you would.' I sat behind you. And when you allowed yourself to slump onto your side your spine touched my rounded belly and I felt the child inside me kick. I still don't know if you felt it too. I rubbed your back. Gently, gently with my right hand, my left elbow resting on your pillow, my left hand on your shoulder. It comforted me so, I could have rubbed for hours.

The doctor with the burning eyes hurries back carrying a hypodermic. He says, 'Like this you are making your blood-pressure go up. I will give you some Valium. Could you please roll up your sleeve?'

With my right hand I roll up my left sleeve.

The Filipino nurse says, 'You want I do this?'

But he does not answer and eases the needle into my arm. The Valium hurts as it enters the muscle. He pulls out the needle and the nurse starts rubbing the tiny puncture with an antiseptic wipe.

'You will sleep now,' he says, and his mouth smiles.

My body is in pieces, each piece too heavy for me to support. My hands are grotesque pads, the now ringless fingers so stiff I wonder at the time when moving them required no conscious thought. The wrists where I used to watch the shadowy pulse throb under transparent skin are now dense, opaque flesh. If I stretch out my arms and hang them through the rails at the sides of the bed they are – for a while – not uncomfortable. The left arm hurts and I have to be careful with it or the drip tubes will get tangled and blocked. My breasts are so heavy they drag at the skin of my chest. I have to wear a bra pulled high and tight. It cuts into my ribs and presses on my lungs. Every few minutes I have to disengage my right hand and lift the elastic and hold it away from me so that I can breathe. When I hang my arm back on the railing the relief of not having to support it rushes through my shoulder and my chest. What will they think when they come in and find me like this: a suffering figure, arms stretched out to the sides? Or do Christian images – even this one – not exist for them at all? They are probably not into images. Our religion is a religion of the Word not the Image. I close my eyes. Relax, they say, relax, worrying is not good for you.

I am alone and this room is not unpleasant. There are no oranges or browns. The walls and bedclothes are white. There is a grey 'incoming calls only' telephone by my bed and my mother, father, family call me from Cairo and my husband from London. There is a grey leather armchair. There is a television on a shelf in the corner and between it and the window there is a bilingual notice. The English says, 'Under no circumstance you must be alone with male doctor. Call sister urgently if male doctor approaches you for examination.' I think this is funny and copy it laboriously into my notepad. I am alone and so, unobserved, I can hold onto what is left of me. Next to the notice I have pinned up the painting of a big, bright butterfly my daughter brought me on her first visit. I keep my exam papers next to me and try to correct them when I can.

In the morning the nurses detach me from the drip and I let myself carefully off the bed. I walk slowly across the room and into the bathroom. I pee with what precision I can into the waiting jug and cover it and replace it on the shelf. Although this is no longer the body I know, I wash it meticulously, spray it with eau de toilette and dab moisturising lotion on the bits I can reach. I brush my hair, and do what I can with my face: I draw a black pencil along the puffy eyelids, apply some mascara and lip-gloss. I put a bedjacket on over my night-dress. Back in the room, the bed has been made and the nurse helps me into it. She twitters that I should not get up, that I should use a bed-pan, that I should let her wash me with a flannel. I smile politely and say nothing. She is very clean and neat with her white linen uniform and her small features and glossy black hair pulled back in a pony-tail. She measures my blood-pressure, my temperature, my pulse, and notes it all down. She re-attaches my drips and I lie back weak and nauseous but ready with my face, my bedjacket, my notepads and exam papers for the doctors' morning rounds.

They sweep into the room and position themselves at the foot of the bed. The consultant, majestic in his white robes and black-and-gold *abaya*, stands centre stage. The nurse hands him the notes and stands back. He looks at them and, slightly behind him, the Indian registrar with slicked back hair and a tightly shuttered face looks at them too. There is another doctor: Sudanese; Othello with a grieving face and a limp and an ebony cane. Three local house-doctors stand further back. They are women and all I can see of them is their dark eyes through the slits of their black veils.

When they go, the Filipino nurse asks if my arm is stiff. She whispers that it was wrong of the doctor to put the Valium in my arm. 'It should be here,' she says, patting my hip, 'but he was afraid to ask you. The muscle in the arm is not so big.'

Your back was so thin, through the flannel night-gown and the woollen cloak, I could feel each vertebra. I rubbed slowly down your spine, and out and up in a circle and pressed your shoulder and your neck, then went down your spine again. I could have cradled you like a baby. I could have kissed your head and your hands and wept over you. But I sat behind you and rubbed your back and thought, tomorrow I leave. Will you still be here when I come back in the summer? I wanted to tell you things, and to ask you things. I said, 'Do you remember when we had lunch at the Meridien seven years ago?'

'You should not go downstairs,' the nurse says at five o'clock as she disengages my drips.

'You don't allow children up here,' I reply. I ease myself off the bed and wrap my body in the black *abaya* and my head in the black *tarha* and walk slowly out of the door.

In the women's corner of the vast waiting-area on the ground floor my daughter climbs onto my knee. She strokes my uncovered face and I bury my mouth in her small, plump palm. She plants big, wet kisses on my eyes, my cheeks, my nose and my mouth. A group of women sitting silently nearby stare at us through their veils.

On my fourth day, the door of my room opens and a woman walks in. She is tall and wears a long, loose grey garment with buttons up the front and the usual black veil over her face and head. In her hand she carries a covered dish. She looks around to make sure I am alone in the room –

'There are no men?'

'There are none.'

She lifts the veil from her face and lays it back on top of her head. 'Peace be upon you!'

'And upon you, peace and the mercy of God and His blessings.'

She puts the dish on the cabinet next to the phone and settles into the grey armchair. She has a young but not particularly fine face. She wears, of course, no make-up.

'I have brought you something to support you, sister. Hospital food is tasteless.'

'May God increase your bounty,' I say; 'it was not necessary to trouble yourself.'

'We see no one comes to visit you?'

'I have no people here.'

As I say the words I feel tears of self-pity well up behind my eyes. But I blink them away. I can do this much.

'They say you are married to an Englishman?'

'It is true.'

'But how can you marry an Englishman?'

'It is my portion and my fate.'

'But you are Muslim. How can you marry an Englishman?'

'He has embraced our religion.'

'And you live there?'

'Yes.'

'How can you live there? They are all animals there.'

'They are people, like us.'

'They live like animals there.'

'They live like us. Among them there is good and there is bad.'

'They copulate on the streets there.'

'Pardon?'

'There, the people copulate on the streets.'

'I have lived there a long time; I never saw anybody copulating on the street.'

'I saw it.'

'Where?'

'In films. My husband brings home video films and I have seen them: the man goes to the woman in the street, he lifts her clothes and copulates with her.'

'Ah! Those films don't represent the truth. They are made only to excite people's appetites.'

'I have to go,' she says, and rises. 'But your husband is a good man? He is good to you?'

'Like my own people.'

'My husband is a teacher.'

'It is a good profession.'

'Peace be upon you!' She pulls the veil down over her face and moves towards the door.

'And upon you, peace,' I say, 'and thank you for your generous gift.'

We had taken refuge from the July heat in the air-conditioned coffee-shop of the Cairo Meridien. We drank chilled white wine and ate tomato and white cheese salad and artichokes vinaigrette. Your first play was a rave and people turned to look again at you as they walked past. We watched the sun sparkle silver on the Nile at its widest point and we peeled the leaves off the artichokes and ate their pale, green hearts and I told you of all the ways I loved him and you listened. Then I told you of how, when I had the flu, he had tended me like a mother. 'He even read me a silly little fairy story,' I said, 'to cheer me up.' You said, 'Marry him.' I said, 'But how will I manage never to speak to him in my own language? How can I stand not to live here?' 'Egypt will always be there for you,' you said.

On the sixth day, the Scottish matron comes in and rechecks my pulse. She says I should have morphine and should not go downstairs any more. I say, 'But you don't allow children up here and I have to see my daughter.'

She says my body is like a compression chamber and every move I make adds to the pressure on my baby.

'What about tension?' I say. 'What about misery? What about loneliness?'

'They are animals these people,' she says, 'animals. They don't understand a thing. They think if they have rules it makes them civilized. But never mind, pet. You just think of your baby and be a good girl and we'll have you out of here very soon.'

My students phone me and send me flowers and fruit. They offer to take my little girl to their houses to swim, to play with their children. But no one can bring her here to me.

My husband phones me every day. He has tried to get a visa to come over but they tell him it has to be sent from this end and will take at least three weeks. 'You'll be out of that damned place by then, won't you?' he says. 'You'll be home.'

I correct my exam papers and after each question I have to stop to take my breath and pluck at the elastic of my bra.

Outside, after I left you, I looked up at your house – your father's house and his father's before him – and it was ablaze with lights. And there in the street, I hugged him, my old friend, your husband, and the doorman turned away and wiped his face with his wide Nubian sleeve.

My mother phones and tells me you have been to America and back and no, you are not better. Do you think of death? You must do. You must know you are dying. Half your stomach taken out, the needle plastered to your hand ready for your next feed. Your brother scouring the medical depots for supplies, your doctors on twenty-four-hour rotas, your family coming and going and no one ever mentioning the dread name of your disease. All the talk was of ulcers and vague complications and exploratory surgery, not of the removal of chunks of stomach and yards of intestine – not of the disease that manoeuvres like mercury, finding fresh footholds as the old are cut away. You must know. Your husband said you did not. He said it was better like this, you would not be able to take it. Is this the last kindness you are doing him, allowing him to believe you do not know? Playing it his way to the end? Letting him off grand finales and anguished summing-ups?

For three days my mother does not call. When, on my tenth day in this room she calls and I ask after you she begs me not to take it too badly, to think of my blood-pressure, to think of my baby, to think of my daughter. Every possible thing was done. There was nothing more anybody could do.

A nurse comes in with the Sudanese doctor. She stands by as he bends over me. He slips his hand under the cover and speaks kindly. 'What are you doing to your blood-pressure? I will try not to hurt you. Yes, you are dilating. We want to try to hurry things up. Your blood-pressure is much too high. It is all this crying. Why do you make yourself so unhappy? But it may still be possible to have a normal delivery.'

'Is the baby all right?' I ask.

'You are in the eighth month. God willing, the baby will be fine.'

He rims between my legs three times with hard fingers and a nurse hurries in to listen with her black box at the wall of my belly.

On the back of your hand I saw the needle go into the blue vein. In my hand all detail has vanished; the tube disappears under a spaghetti junction of bloodied plasters. I lie and listen out for the movements of my baby, for the little left hooks to my liver, or the flurry of kicks that precedes him falling asleep in a tight ball that wrenches my whole body to one side. He does not move and I imagine him gasping for breath as the cord that connects us fails to deliver the oxygen he needs. No, as *I* fail to deliver the oxygen he needs. I carefully disengage my arm from the railing and rub slowly along the side of my belly, coaxing him, willing him to wake, to kick. I try not to think of you and, as I cast about for other thoughts, I feel the tears on my face while image after unbearable image presents itself to my mind. Five years ago, sitting in the Paprika with my husband when he was still in love with me, he caught my hand across the table and raised it to his mouth. In the car, in the desert, he pushed his hand between my thighs – I want, I want to be five years old and playing in the sunshine on my grandmother's carpet. I want to be at my nineteenth birthday party with all my friends and you, newly-wed, dancing into the room with an armful of white lilies and blue iris. I want to be home. When I turn my head I see, out of the window, a woman cross the car-park in the glaring sun. Her black *abaya* billows out around her and she clutches at it and bends forward as she fights the dust-laden wind.

In the dead of night my phone rings. As I reach for it in the dark I try to still my heart, for I imagine each startled beat adding to the pressure on my baby. What more can happen now? A man's voice, speaking low, calls me by name. An admirer, he says, a well-wisher, one of your doctors, he says. If he spoke in Arabic I could tell which one by his accent but he speaks only English to me. He says, 'I know you cannot leave your bed. Would you like me to be with you? Your breasts are very big now, they hurt you, don't they? If I suck them I can make them better –' I put the phone down and he rings again, and again. I keep the phone off the hook, but if my daughter needs me, if something should happen – I put the receiver back.

When it came, it came suddenly, just as my neighbour – my saviour it turns out – had said it would. How could I, who had been stalked for so long, still be taken so completely by surprise?

On the eleventh day, my daughter on the phone asked, 'Do you still like the butterfly I gave you?'

'Yes, darling,' I said.

'Will it always be nice for you?' she asked.

'Of course it will,' I said.

'And you won't ever hate it *ever*, will you?'

'Of course not, sweetheart,' I said. 'I adore it.'

I turned my head to negotiate the tubes and replace the receiver and felt a muffled rush as though I sensed a distant sea breaking against rock. As the receiver dropped I was pushed under by the rushing waves.

Of the time after, fragments only remain. My teeth chattering so hard that my skull reverberated with the sound. Cloth wedged into my mouth then removed as I started to retch. My stomach empty but a thin stream of bile continuing to eject itself in bitter spurts through my throat. The wetness flowing from me, whether it was water or blood I never knew. The rhythmic blows behind my eyes and voices talking to me, and hands, hands holding, mopping, wiping, carrying me. And then a room with a fierce white light and Othello and the mad-eyed Syrian and other figures busy around me and a churning and grinding kneading my body from waist to groin and needles going into my arms and back and a voice in my ear saying, 'Your husband is on the phone. He wants you to know that he is with you always,' and a matador in overalls and a mask and shower-cap braced between my legs and the white light burning, burning into all the pain and noise until an angel in a black veil dimmed it and turned it away from my face and came and bent over me and I must have said something for she said, 'Have courage, sister. I shall not leave you,' and she held my hand and the ankle of one splayed leg and every time I slipped under that roaring tide I floated up again to hear her soft recitative; her unending verses of Qur'ānic comfort.

He fought his way out, my brave baby boy, and they took him away to an incubator, warm and silent and still as I could not be. And they worked hard at me for what I later learned were three nights and three days until at last, as I lay once again in my old bed, empty and clean and calm, they delivered to me a warm, soft bundle. And holding it close, I folded back the flowered wrappings and saw for myself the breathing brown body, the cut cord, the downy head, the long, black lashes, the curled fingers and my name on the tab around his wrist.

My daughter on the phone says, 'Tomorrow we're coming to get you.'

I say, 'I know. I can't wait.'

'Have you finished your exams?' she asks.

'Yes,' I say, 'they're done.'

'Then we can go home,' she says, 'because we have to show the baby to Daddy.'

'Absolutely,' I say, 'absolutely, sweetheart.'

In the Meridien, all those years ago, with the Nile shining behind you, I said, 'But you've been married nine years. Can one trust passion – romance? Can one really trust being in love?' A shadow passed across your face. 'Well,' you said, after a moment, 'of course things change. Yes, they do. But, I think now, perhaps, sympathy – yes, sympathy and kindness and good-will. *They* can last, if we're wise. Maybe they are the lasting part of love. My husband has those. And your man, from what you say, has them too.'

You had everything I wanted: confidence, high cheek-bones, a long-running play, a happy – well, comparatively happy – second marriage. I think of you on Friday nights, the door of your lit-up house open onto the garden, the garden gate open onto the road. You move between your guests, your husband, your pets, your children, your mother, your servants. You make conversation, drinks and food, and I watch you lightly draw the fine-lined patterns that pull so many lives together. My dear – oh, my dear, you made it look so easy.

A NOTE ON THE AUTHOR

Ahdaf Soueif was born in Cairo and
educated in Egypt and England. She is the
author of *Aisha*, and *In the Eye of the Sun*.